# The New Girl

# From the Chicken House

It's lovely to be back with my favourite girl gang (apart from the Chicken House team, of course!) in another wonderful adventure. They are still being bothered by those annoying boys, but this time there's a new girl to help!

Barry Cunningham
Publisher

# Cornelia Funke

# The New Girl

**Translated from the German
by Oliver Latsch**

Chicken House

2 Palmer Street, Frome, Somerset BA11 1DS
www.doublecluck.com

Original © Cornelia Funke 1996
English translation © Oliver Latsch 2012

First published in Germany as *Die Wilden Hühner auf Klassenfahrt*
by Cecile Dressler Verlag GmbH & Co. KG, Hamburg, 1996

Published in Great Britain in 2012
The Chicken House
2 Palmer Street
Frome, Somerset BA11 1DS
United Kingdom
www.doublecluck.com

Cover and interior design by Steve Wells
Cover illustration by Linzie Hunter
Typeset by Dorchester Typesetting Group Ltd
Printed and bound in Great Britain by CPI Group (UK) Ltd, Croydon, CR0 4YY

The paper used in this Chicken House book is made from wood
grown in sustainable forests.

1 3 5 7 9 10 8 6 4 2

British Library Cataloguing in Publication data available.

ISBN 978-1-904442-87-5

*For Frederik, Anne, Simone, Sebastian,*
*Lina, Katharina, Hannes, Tina*
*and all the other C.H.I.X. and Piranhas*

## Chapter One

'In here! Quick!' shouted Charlie, pressing the button to open the train door. 'Hurry!'

She threw her bag on to one of the seats, put her jacket on another and plonked herself down on the seat by the window.

'Hey, what's the rush?' moaned Xa, her overstuffed rucksack briefly getting stuck in the carriage door. Xa, short for Alexandra, was Charlie's best friend.

'Where are the others?' asked Charlie. She was talking about Izzie and Hannah, the rest of their gang, the C.H.I.X. They had called themselves that after the the first letters of their names and the chickens that Charlie sometimes had to look after.

'Coming,' answered Xa. She heaved the rucksack on to the luggage rack.

'Put your jacket on that empty seat there,' said Charlie. A few boys from their class squeezed down the aisle next to them. Freddie stuck his tongue out at Xa, while Tom and Olly pulled faces at her.

'Look at those idiots!' giggled Xa. She made her most horrible face back, all squinty-eyed. The boys barged their way into the next carriage, hammering tables as they passed. 'Right,' said Xa, dropping into her seat. 'All the Piranhas are here. Except for Will, but he'll probably show up soon.' Olly, Freddie, Will and Tom were the C.H.I.X.'s biggest rivals, known as the Piranhas.

'Great . . .' muttered Charlie. She put her long legs up on the seat opposite.

Someone else got on the train. Isobel, also known as Gorgeous Izzie, popped her head round the carriage door. 'How about it? Room for two more C.H.I.X.?'

'Come on in!' said Charlie. 'Is Hannah with you?'

'Of course.' Izzie nudged a huge travel bag through the door.

'Morning,' mumbled Hannah, sleepily.

'Oof!' Charlie helped Izzie lug the massive bag on to the luggage rack. 'What have you got in there? Your entire make-up collection, or something?'

'Ha, ha!' Izzie sat down next to Xa and flicked her blonde hair off her face. 'Clothes, of course. You never know what the weather'll be like.'

Charlie shrugged. 'Just as long as you've got your necklace.'

'Well, what do *you* think?' Izzie pulled out the chicken feather that hung on a chain around her neck. The others all had them, too, only they wore theirs on leather thongs. The feather necklace was their C.H.I.X. badge, and only they could wear one.

'I think we're off,' said Hannah.

The train gave a lurch and slowly pulled out of the gloomy station into the sunlight.

'Fab weather for going on a school trip, isn't it?' Izzie produced a bag of gummy bears from her pocket and offered it round. Charlie and Xa helped themselves, but Hannah shook her head. 'No, thanks. I'm trying to eat a bit less.'

'Since when?' asked Charlie.

'Since two days ago.' Embarrassed, Hannah tugged at her ponytail. 'Well, I thought I'd better, what with all the food we'll be getting.' Charlie looked out of the window and wrote her name on the dusty glass with her finger. The train rolled over a railway bridge. Beneath them the river glittered in the sunlight. 'You know what? I'm getting quite excited now.'

'Really? Yesterday you were trying to make us all pretend to be ill so we could stay at home,' said Xa.

'I know,' replied Charlie. 'But that was yesterday . . .'

Next door, the Piranhas were singing football songs.

'Completely talentless,' said Izzie. 'I know! Let's sing something too!'

Charlie groaned. 'Oh no! Spare us, please.'

'Izzie has a good voice,' said Hannah, loyally. 'She's in the choir. First soprano.' Hannah was Izzie's best friend and Izzie could do no wrong in her eyes.

'I know she is!' Charlie screwed up her face. 'But if she starts singing now, I'll jump out the window.'

Izzie had just opened her mouth to make a not-so-friendly reply when the carriage doors hissed open again.

'The ticket inspector!' whispered Hannah, panicking. 'Oh no! Where did I put my ticket?'

But it was only Tom, the smallest and loudest member of the Piranhas.

'Hello, Chickens!' he yelled. 'Got a message for you.'

He threw a rolled-up piece of paper into Xa's lap. Then, with a grin, he slammed the door shut again.

'Oh!' Izzie screwed up her eyes. 'Ha ha, I bet Tom fancies Xa again.'

'Rubbish!' muttered Xa. But her face had flushed bright red.

'He wrote love letters to Izzie as well!' said Hannah.

'That was ages ago,' said Charlie. 'Come on, Xa, read it.'

Reluctantly, Xa unrolled the paper. The other C.H.I.X. leant forward.

'That's no love letter,' announced Charlie. 'That's Freddie's scrawl.'

Freddie was the leader of the Piranhas.

'"Warning to the C.H.I.C.K.S",' read Xa. 'Honestly! He can't even spell 'C.H.I.X.' properly.'

'What warning?' asked Hannah. She fiddled with her glasses uneasily.

'Hang on.' Xa smoothed out the paper. 'It's not easy reading Freddie's terrible writing. "We, the Piranhas, hereby announce that the *piece treety* with the stupid *Chicks* does not count in other places. So be on your *gard*, Chicks! Signed: The Piranhas.'"

Xa looked up. 'Oh no, not all that again!'

'I knew it!' said Charlie, gleefully. She rubbed her hands together. 'They're so going to regret this!'

'But the treaty still holds on the boat, doesn't it?' Hannah asked. Just thinking about the ferry trip to St Peter's Island made her feel seasick. 'I don't want them to steal my sick bags. I get really ill.'

Charlie nodded. 'That's only fair. I'll check with Freddie.'

'Perhaps ferries don't roll about that much,' said Xa.

Hannah just managed a weak smile.

Chapter Two

**H**annah did get seasick. Even though the sea was quite calm that day, and even though the old ferry they were on did not roll at all.

But she was not alone. Mrs Rose, their teacher, also kept disappearing off to the toilets and Olly, the Piranhas' magician, could not complete a single card trick. His face had turned as green as the cafeteria floor.

And while Hannah spent the crossing in the smelly toilets, Izzie hung out with Freddie and Tom by the slot machines. Considering their peace treaty was over, Charlie found this inexcusable, but she wasn't in the mood to get cross. Instead, she joined Xa up on deck. They looked at the sea and let the salty air blow in their faces, and enjoyed themselves. Xa was glad to be away from home for a few days. Since her mother had gone back to work Xa had to look after her little brother even more than before. And Charlie thought nothing could beat leaning on a ship's rails with her best friend, looking out over the sea.

'It wouldn't be too bad being a seagull, would it?' said Xa. 'I think I'd like that.'

'But then you'd have to eat raw fish all day.' Charlie leant over the rusty guard rail. 'I think I'd rather be a pirate. On a big ship, with the sails above me creaking in the wind, and the ropes rattling. I'd sleep in the crow's nest every night, until I knew all the stars by heart.'

'That sounds pretty good too,' sighed Xa. She squinted into the sun. 'Look there, dead ahead. I think that's our island.'

A coach was waiting for them when they got off the ferry, and by the time they pulled up in front of the youth hostel, it was early afternoon.

Mrs Rose's legs were still a little wobbly from the crossing, but she managed to gather her whole class around her. Mr Dudman was standing off to the side, looking bored as usual.

'Right!' Mrs Rose's voice was a little shaky too. 'Our rooms are on the first floor, on the corridor to the right. No pushing, no shoving – there's a bed for everyone. Take your things up to your room in a calm and orderly fashion, and then we'll meet down in the entrance hall at four for a little stroll on the beach. OK?'

'"A little stroll on the beach"!' Tom pulled a face. 'Sounds thrilling.'

Mrs Rose just looked at him and he immediately fell silent. She was good at that.

'What about food?' asked Olly. His face had returned to its normal pink.

'Lunch is served at one o'clock sharp,' said Mrs Rose. 'So we missed it today. That's why you were all supposed to bring a packed lunch.'

'I already ate that,' said Olly, miserably.

'And puked it up again!' chipped in Freddie, grinning broadly.

'Well, you're not going to starve to death, Olly,' growled Will. 'All that flab should keep you going till dinner.'

Olly blushed and Mrs Rose clapped her hands.

'That's enough!' she said. 'Off to your rooms, all of you. Mr Dudman and I will do an inspection later.'

'Come on!' said Charlie to the other C.H.I.X. 'The first room is ours.'

They ran as fast as they could, which, thanks to Izzie's huge bag, wasn't fast enough. Hannah helped her friend carry it, but they were still overtaken on the stairs. By the time the C.H.I.X. got to the corridor, the first room was already taken. The next one, too, already had two boys in it.

Fighting for breath, Charlie raced into the third room.

'What? Six beds!' she yelled. 'Do they all have six beds?'

Xa and Izzie followed her in and looked around.

'Well, I'm sleeping on a top bunk,' said Izzie. 'I won't be able to breathe on the bottom.'

'Me too.' Charlie dragged her bag over to a top bunk by the window. 'OK?'

'I don't care either way,' said Xa. She put her rucksack down.

'Where's Hannah?' asked Charlie, anxiously. A couple of kids had already put their heads around the door, but no one had yet tried to claim the three remaining beds.

'Hannah's bag fell open,' said Izzie sticking a piece of chewing gum in her mouth. 'Right on the stairs. She's probably still picking up all her things.'

'What? And you just left her there?' said Xa. 'After she helped you with your huge bag?'

'I had to get mine to the room first!' cried Izzie, indignantly.

'Honestly!' exclaimed Xa. '*I'll* go and help her!' She ran to the door.

'And how exactly am I supposed to save all these beds?' Charlie shouted after her.

'You'll manage,' answered Xa. And then she was gone.

Izzie and Charlie looked at each other.

'Don't look at me like that!' huffed Izzie. 'It's not my fault!'

The door opened again. Three girls from their class peered inside.

'Have you got any beds left?' one of them asked shyly. Her name was Amy. Standing next to her was Helena, who was new to their class.

'Of course they're free,' said Ellie, the third girl. She pushed her way past the others into the room.

'No, they're not!' Angrily, Charlie planted herself in Ellie's path. 'Xa and Hannah are still coming.'

'So?' Ellie threw her bag on to the free top bunk. 'That still leaves two beds. Even a bird-brain can work that out.'

Charlie pursed her lips. Izzie said nothing.

'Here we are!' said Xa, pulling a panting Hannah into the room.

'You see?' Charlie folded her arms. 'Those two beds belong to us. One of you has to go.'

Helena and Amy looked at each other. 'I'm not leaving,' said Helena. 'The only other free bed is next door. I'm not going in there with those meanies. They've been picking on me all day.'

'Well, I'm really sorry, but one of you will have to go in with them.' Charlie took Hannah's bag and threw it on to the bunk beneath Izzie's.

'I could go,' said Izzie who was brushing her hair. 'I don't mind.'

'What?' Charlie looked at her, dumbfounded. 'We swore to stay together. Have you forgotten that already?'

'Swore? How sweet!' Ellie pulled a face. She took a magazine out of her bag and settled down on her bed. 'Of course, the four of you are in a gang, aren't you? The T.W.I.T.S. or something.'

Charlie shot her an angry look.

Helena and Amy were still standing in the doorway.

'It's OK,' murmured Amy. 'I'll go.'

Without glancing at the others she dragged her bag back out into the hall. Then she quietly shut the door behind her.

Xa gave Charlie a withering look. 'Couldn't you have been a bit nicer? She's all alone now. And she has to go in with that lot and listen to their endless meanness.'

'They're not that bad,' said Izzie.

'Oh yeah?' Charlie looked at her. 'Well, you certainly seemed quite happy to share with them.'

'Stop arguing!' shouted Hannah, her eyes filling with tears. Hannah got upset easily.

Helena put her bag on the bunk beneath Ellie's and sat down next to it. She beamed at them.

'You know what?' she said, bouncing up and down on her mattress. 'I was hoping I'd end up in your room.

I really, really want to join your gang!'

Charlie frowned at her. 'Oh yeah? Well, that's just not possible. Four in the gang is enough. And anyway . . .' she rubbed her nose, '. . . you'd have to survive at least one adventure before you could become one of us. A test, you know?'

'What test?' asked Hannah, baffled. 'I never did—'

Charlie shot her a warning glance, and Hannah shut up quickly.

'Thing is, Helena,' said Izzie, jumping down from her bunk. 'Being one of the C.H.I.X. isn't the greatest thing in the world . . .'

Charlie looked as if she was going to explode.

'Although,' continued Izzie with a smile, 'we do have fun. A lot of fun! Like when we go fishing.'

'Fishing?' Helena looked puzzled.

'For Piranhas,' explained Izzie.

The other C.H.I.X. grinned. Oh yes, they all remembered that adventure! And the Piranhas would never forget it either, for as long as they lived. It was unbelievable that they'd dared to break the peace treaty after being so completely beaten.

'Where have the Piranhas got to, anyway?' asked Charlie.

'We should check,' said Xa.

Helena jumped up from her bed. 'Can I come with you?' she asked.

'No!' said Charlie. She opened the door.

Izzie poked her head into the corridor. 'It's all clear out here.'

'Then let's go!' whispered Charlie.

As quietly as mice, the C.H.I.X. crept into the hall.

Ellie didn't stir from behind her magazine, but Helena watched them go, green with envy.

Chapter Three

The Piranhas were in a room with four beds at the end of the corridor, right by the bathrooms. Finding them was easy for the C.H.I.X., as they'd left their door wide open and Tom's voice could be heard all the way down the corridor. As usual, he was loudly telling jokes that only he found funny.

Well, jokes that Xa sometimes found funny too. Just as she did now.

'Stop giggling!' whispered Charlie as they tiptoed towards the open door.

'Sorry!' Xa whispered back, starting again.

'You'd better stay here with Hannah, then,' hissed Charlie. 'You two can find out where the teachers' rooms are. Izzie, you're with me.'

The two girls moved on soundlessly, until they stood

by the Piranhas' door.

'Hey, watch this,' announced Olly. 'I've got a new trick.'

'Sorry, Ol, seen that one already,' said Freddie. 'Will, shut the door. Time to decide what to do about those annoying C.H.I.X.!'

Izzie and Charlie heard him coming and pressed themselves as tightly as they could against the wall outside.

'Hey,' they heard Will say. 'I know that stink . . .'

In a second, he was in the corridor. 'Hello, Izzie,' he said, with his best Frankenstein grin. 'I knew I recognised that girly perfume. Hey, Freddie, check out who's been spying on us.'

'Don't flatter yourselves!' Charlie did her best to look straight through the boys. 'We were just going to the bathroom.'

'Is that right?' asked Freddie. 'Well, you've walked right past it. Maybe you should call yourselves the four blind M.I.C.E.'

'You know what we do with spies, don't you?' asked Will.

Izzie yawned. 'I haven't got a clue, Will,' she said. 'What *do* you do with spies?' She lazily blew a chewing-gum bubble and let it burst right in front of his nose. Charlie looked at her in admiration – Izzie wasn't scared of anything! And Will wasn't known for his sense of humour.

'If you weren't a girl,' he growled, 'I'd . . .'

'Leave it,' said Freddie, pulling him back.

Izzie just gave the boys a big smile, linked arms with Charlie and vanished into the bathroom with her friend.

'Izzie!' Charlie pulled her arm free. 'Do you have to wear so much of that stuff all the time? We could've found out what they're planning if you hadn't given us away.'

Izzie shrugged. She was looking in the mirror. 'So? Not knowing kind of makes things more interesting, don't you think?'

She pulled a little brush from her pocket and started tidying her hair. Charlie looked at her, dumbstruck.

'What happened?' Hannah came panting into the bathroom. 'We saw them catch you!'

Charlie nodded. 'And all because Izzie likes to smell like a walking perfume counter. Still, at least we know where their room is.'

'The teachers' rooms are by the stairs,' said Hannah. 'Right at the beginning of the corridor. We could hear Mr Dudman's radio through the door. And Mrs Rose has hung her name on the door handle.'

Izzie finished brushing her hair. 'Where's Xa?' she asked.

'She wanted to see if Amy was OK,' replied Hannah. 'She feels bad about the whole room thing.'

'Tell her I need the baby monitor,' said Charlie. 'Right away.'

'What baby monitor?' asked Izzie.

'I got Xa to bring her little brother's spare baby monitor,' answered Charlie. 'As soon as the boys go downstairs I'll sneak into their room and hide it somewhere. You just have to make sure they don't come back up again before I'm done.'

'OK, but what's the baby monitor for?' said Hannah.

'So we can listen to the Piranhas!' explained Charlie. 'The sound isn't great, but it'll do. Xa and I tried it out at home.'

Izzie grinned. 'Excellent!' She looked at her watch. 'We have to be downstairs for Mrs Rose in ten minutes. Don't be late. You know how she hates it if we're late.'

Charlie nodded. 'No worries. Just tell Xa to find me here.'

Barely a minute later Charlie heard someone hurrying down the corridor.

She jumped off the bathroom window ledge where she had almost got comfortable, and then froze.

'Hi, Xa,' she heard Tom say. It sounded as if he was standing right outside the bathroom door.

'Oh, hi!' answered Xa, a little breathlessly.

'How, er . . .' Tom cleared his throat. 'How's your room?'

Charlie put her ear to the door. What on earth was he up to?

'Good,' said Xa. 'We can see the sea.'

'Great,' replied Tom. 'I wish we had a view. I like the sea.

Charlie looked at her watch. Nearly four. How long were those two going to stand there?

'What's that you've got?' she heard Tom ask. Oh no – the baby monitor. Xa was a hopeless liar.

'That? Oh, er . . .' Xa started stuttering. 'That's, er, that's the charger for – for my electric toothbrush.'

'Oh, right,' said Tom. 'Well, I'd best be off. See ya round, then, yeah? I'll buy you an ice cream if you like.'

'OK,' said Xa.

Then the door banged open and Xa rushed headlong into the bathroom.

'What took you so long?' Charlie hissed. 'I've been standing here so long my feet are killing me!'

'Well, what was I supposed to do? I couldn't just ignore him.' She handed Charlie the baby monitor. 'There you go.'

'"Charger for my electric toothbrush"?' Charlie giggled. 'Not bad, I suppose. But now can you go downstairs and tell Mrs Rose I'm still in the loo?'

'Will do,' said Xa. 'See you later, and good luck!' Then she was gone.

## Chapter Four

The weather was still perfect as Mrs Rose led the whole class down to the beach. Mr Dudman was trudging along, bringing up the rear. Every now and then he glanced at the sea as if that bored him too.

Charlie's lateness had earned her a telling-off from Mrs Rose, but it didn't seem to have made the Piranhas suspicious. Charlie had found the perfect socket for the baby monitor – right next to Freddie's bed. And now it was waiting there, switched on behind a curtain. Charlie could hardly wait.

'It's so beautiful, isn't it?' said Xa, unable to take her eyes off the sea and nearly falling over her own feet.

'Sorry?' muttered Hannah. 'Oh, yeah, great.' She was starving, nibbling unhappily on an apple, while just a few steps ahead Olly tucked into a bag of crisps.

Izzie didn't look too happy, either. 'This wind is so annoying!' she moaned. 'It feels as if it's blowing into one ear and right out the other.'

'Put a hat on,' said Charlie, unsympathetically. 'You won't look so good, but your ears will stay warm.'

Izzie ignored her.

'Hey, Charlie!' Helena was tugging on her sleeve. 'Look what I made,' she said, proudly holding out a string with a feather on it, which she was wearing around her neck.

Charlie squinted at it crossly. 'Hey!' she exclaimed. 'Only real C.H.I.X. are allowed to wear one of those. Take it off!'

Helena looked stung, and quickly tucked the feather back under her jumper.

'No!' she said. 'It's only a gull's feather, and you can't stop me from wearing one of those, can you?'

Xa grinned, and Hannah chuckled sympathetically. Charlie shot them both a glare.

Helena tugged at her sleeve again. 'Come on, Charlie!' she said, again. How about I spy a little for you? Or keep watch? You can never have enough look-outs.'

'No thanks!' snapped Charlie. She started to walk faster but Helena managed to keep up, even though Charlie's legs were nearly twice as long as hers. The others were still giggling.

'Look, just forget it, will you!' Charlie snapped. 'Our gang is full.'

Helena looked around before lowering her voice. 'But if *I* spied on the Piranhas,' she whispered, 'they wouldn't suspect anything.'

'She's got a point,' said Izzie.

'A *good* point!' said Hannah, enthusiastically. She went to throw her apple core into the sea, but missed and hit Olly on the back of the head instead. She gasped and quickly ducked out of sight when he looked around.

'The spying is sorted,' growled Charlie at the others. 'The baby monitor—'

'It can't hurt to let her try,' interrupted Xa. 'Those monitors crackle a lot, and the boys could easily find it.'

'All right!' shrugged Charlie. 'But that doesn't mean you're one of us.'

'Oh, thanks!' whispered Helena. 'That is super cool! I'll get to work right away.'

She looked around. Will and Tom had rolled up their trousers and were splashing about in the icy-cold water, trying to soak anyone who came too close. Hardly ideal for a spy. So Helena glued herself to Freddie instead. He was collecting shells and stones, stuffing what he found into Olly's backpack. Helena was following him so closely she had to be careful not to bump into him.

'Look at her!' giggled Izzie. 'Helena: our new secret weapon.'

'Hey, there's Amy,' said Xa. 'I think I'll go and say hello.' She skipped off across the sand to where Amy was walking along the beach by herself. Immediately, Tom stopped chasing Will, and sauntered over to the two girls.

'See!' Izzie nudged Charlie. 'I was right, after all! He *is* after Xa. Probably because she's the only one who laughs at his stupid jokes.'

Charlie narrowed her eyes. 'Or maybe he just wants to cosy up to her, find out about our plans.'

'Charlie!' Izzie rolled her eyes. 'You really are clueless. Not everyone takes this gang stuff as seriously as you do.'

'Don't they?' Charlie looked hurt. 'Aren't you having fun?'

'Of course I am!' Izzie brushed her windswept hair from her face. 'But *that*,' she pointed at Tom and Xa, 'has nothing to do with the gang. OK, look, I bet you two packs of chewing gum that tomorrow she'll have a note from him.'

'OK. You're on.' Charlie bent down and picked up a shell. They were really quite pretty. Maybe she'd collect a few, they'd make the room back at the hostel look nice. Which reminded her . . . 'The boys are lucky,' she mumbled, looking out at the sea with a gloomy face.

'They have a room to themselves. And we're stuck with Helena and Ellie. We can't even have a proper C.H.I.X. chat in there.'

'Of course we can. Helena totally hero-worships you, and Ellie . . .' Izzie picked up a few pebbles and threw them into the water. 'Ellie doesn't care about any of that stuff, anyway. To her we're all just a bunch of stupid babies that she's stuck with.'

'Why?' asked Charlie. 'What's her problem, anyway?'

'She's cross because she had to repeat a year,' said Hannah. 'She just hangs out with the other two who had to stay down as well, and thinks she's far too grown-up for the likes of us.'

'Hmm,' grumbled Charlie. She'd still rather have a room with just four beds.

They'd been trudging through the wet sand for ages when they saw Mr Dudman, striding out to catch up with Mrs Rose. Smiling at last, he pointed at his watch to tell her that it was time to head back. The sun hung low over the sea. The tide was going out and the water had shrunk back from the beach.

'I was beginning to think old Rosey was going to make us walk all the way to the horizon!' groaned Hannah. 'I can barely lift my feet, I'm so tired. And hungry! I hope it's not going to be like this every day, I'll go mad.'

'Oh, there'll be lots of walking,' said Izzie. 'Beach walks, night walks, dune walks . . .'

Hannah sighed.

The Piranhas seemed to be tired out too. They were shambling along the beach with Felix and Josh, the two biggest show-offs in the class.

Helena had given up on any more spying and had rejoined the C.H.I.X. – inconspicuously, of course. Pretending her shoelace had come undone, she crouched down between Charlie and Izzie. 'Felix is telling some diving story,' she whispered. 'He's escaped killer sharks three times, apparently. And before he started boasting, they were just droning on about football, unless FA and Man U are code words for something else?'

'Nope.' Izzie popped another piece of chewing gum into her mouth. 'I don't think so.'

'You sure?' asked Charlie.

Izzie grinned. 'Positive.'

'Shame,' muttered Helena. She looked crestfallen. 'Shall I try again?'

'No, leave it,' said Charlie. 'We're nearly back at the hostel anyway.' She looked around.

Xa wasn't far behind, still walking and chatting with Amy. Charlie was surprised to find that she felt a little bit jealous. Just a tiny bit.

\* \* \*

It was nearly six when they got to the hostel. After dinner, Mrs Rose assembled them all at the bottom of the stairs again.

'The evening is yours,' she announced. 'The games room, which has table football and ping-pong, will be open until nine. At nine o'clock sharp you will all be back in your rooms, please. Mr Dudman and I will be checking up on you. Lights out at ten. Breakfast is at seven-thirty.'

'Seven-thirty?' Olly cried out. 'I thought this was a holiday!'

'Seven-thirty,' repeated Mrs Rose. 'We'll wake you at seven. That will be Mr Dudman's job.'

Mr Dudman smiled as he produced a whistle and held it up in the air.

'Furthermore,' continued Mrs Rose, 'there will be no flooding of the bathrooms, no sneaking along the corridors after ten, and no, I repeat, *no* outings to the beach unaccompanied by a teacher at any point on this trip. Is that clear?'

'Yes, Miss,' muttered the class.

Mr Dudman cleared his throat. 'And no childish pranks, if you please. Like toothpaste on the door handles of the teachers' bedrooms.'

'Is using sunscreen more grown-up, Sir?' asked Tom.

The others all sniggered. Mr Dudman just rolled his eyes.

Chapter
Five

The Piranhas played table football in the games room from six until nine. Without a break. They also devoured bags of crisps, yelled 'Goal!' every five minutes, and called each other stupid football nicknames, such Tommo or Ollster. In fact, they generally behaved as if the C.H.I.X. did not exist.

Charlie was fed up, but Izzie, Hannah and Xa were more than happy. They wanted to have a girls' evening in their bedroom, with tea and biscuits. Only Helena understood Charlie's disappointment. She suggested they at least put some of the mushy peas from dinner in the boys' beds, but only Charlie thought that was a good idea.

Then, just as they'd convinced the other three to pay a little visit to the Piranhas' bedroom, Olly came up to practise some magic tricks on his own in there.

'Typical!' muttered Charlie. The C.H.I.X. and Helena were all sitting on their beds, while Ellie had stayed downstairs. 'That idiot Olly! You know what he's trying to do right now? Make a ball disappear under a towel. But he keeps dropping it on the floor!'

'Oh, stop being so grumpy.' Izzie looked around. 'Where did you put the tea tins?'

'By the window.' Thanks to Grandma Slater, the C.H.I.X. were now tea experts.

'Vanilla, Rose Leaf,' read out Izzie. 'Tropical Fire, Cornish Blend. Which do you want?'

'Cornish,' said Xa. 'That sounds cosy.'

The baby monitor crackled. Olly must have dropped his ball again. They heard him swearing under his breath.

While Izzie went off to boil the kettle, Hannah put five big mugs on the table. Five. Helena beamed.

After an eternity, Izzie returned. 'I couldn't do it any quicker,' she said, putting the steaming teapot on the table. 'Mrs Rose was in there.'

She passed the mugs around. Helena pressed hers to her cheek. 'Oh, this is so lovely!' she sighed. 'Being in a gang really is the best thing in the world.'

Charlie shot her a dark look. 'This is so not what a gang is about.' She stirred her tea grumpily. 'If Olly's going to practise his tricks again tomorrow then we'll have to find a way to get him out of that room. Maybe we could think of something now?'

'Oh, come on, Charlie!' Izzie dug in her bag. She produced a packet of biscuits and put it on the table. 'This is our first evening here. Just forget about the boys for once. It's pretty obvious they've forgotten all about us.'

'Exactly,' said Hannah. 'It's great being here, isn't it? I'm not even homesick or anything. Is anyone else?'

Izzie and Helena shook their heads.

'Homesick? What, like, for my gran?' Charlie sipped her tea and looked out of the window. 'Not even slightly.'

Charlie spent a lot of time at her gran's, because her mother worked long hours driving her taxi. Grandma Slater was a stern, unfriendly woman, although she had taught Charlie a lot about tea, and growing vegetables, and keeping chickens!

'I miss my little brother,' said Xa, 'because he's so sweet and cuddly just before bedtime. But apart from that I really like it here.'

'I just hope,' said Izzie, climbing into her bed, 'that none of you snore.'

Hannah blushed, but said nothing.

Suddenly Helena hissed: 'Listen!'

It was just before nine.

The baby monitor crackled briefly, but that wasn't what Helena had heard. There was someone out in the corridor. The wooden floor creaked and the girls stared at the door hardly breathing. Then the handle moved. Thank goodness Charlie had locked it!

'Hey, open up!' someone whispered. 'It's me, Ellie. Let me in!'

Charlie leapt off her bed and ran to the door, her socks making no sound on the polished floor.

'Sorry, Ellie,' she was about to say, when she was squirted in the face by a stream of cold water, accompanied by loud sniggers.

'Got you!' Will shouted gleefully.

'Now you won't need to wash before bed!' called Olly.

Charlie slammed the door shut. Could things get any worse?

Then they really did hear Ellie's voice. 'Let me through, you idiots. And grow up, will you! Put that water pistol away.' Ellie rattled the door handle. 'Hey, twits, open up. Now!'

'We can't!' Helena tried to explain. 'The boys will get in.'

'If you mean your boyfriends who were hanging around here just now, Mrs Rose and Mr Dudman have frightened them off.'

'They're not our boyfriends!' said Charlie, unlocking the door. 'Those are the Piranhas.'

Ellie snorted. 'Yeah? Really scary.'

She climbed into her bunk and grabbed one of her magazines.

'Do you want some tea?' asked Hannah helpfully.

'No, thanks!' answered Ellie. 'What's that terrible noise?'

'The baby monitor!' The C.H.I.X. quickly gathered around the small speaker.

'So, Olly?' asked Freddie. 'What have the C.H.I.X. been up to?' Then there was a crackle and a bang.

'If they're going to lock their door every evening, we'll have to try another time to . . .' Another loud bang.

'Hey, Tom!' yelled Will. 'Stop mucking around in the top bunk, OK? Your mattress keeps bashing into my head.' Another crackle. 'So, anyway, how far did you get with Xa?'

Hannah giggled.

Xa jumped up and yanked the monitor out of its socket. 'Enough!' she said. 'This is stupid. Bugging other people's rooms. It's disgusting!'

She flung the monitor into her bag and threw herself on to her bed.

'I'd say,' said Ellie from behind her magazine, 'the whole gang thing is *really* stupid.'

'It's none of your business!' Charlie snapped.

A gloomy silence fell, before being broken by another

knock on the door.

'Is everything all right with you girls?' asked Mrs Rose, poking her head into the room.

The girls nodded glumly.

Mrs Rose looked sceptical. 'It's not the cheeriest of moods in here, is it?'

'We'll sort it out,' said Izzie.

'OK,' said Mrs Rose. 'But if you don't, or if anyone gets homesick or anything else, you know where I am. Mr Dudman will blow his whistle just before lights out at ten, so don't forget to brush your teeth or you'll be doing it in the dark. Have a good night. You'll see, the sea air quite wipes you out.'

'Goodnight,' mumbled the girls.

And then they were alone again.

Izzie, Hannah, Helena and Charlie played cards until ten. Xa stayed lying on her bed, with her back to them, reading a book. The Piranhas came to the door three more times. They even started poking around in the lock with something. But when Mr Dudman caught them and frogmarched them back to their room, the girls were finally left in peace.

Chapter
Six

That first night Charlie couldn't sleep. She sat up on her bed, clutching the fluffy chicken that went everywhere with her, and looked out at the sea.

Charlie's mum always said she couldn't sleep when the moon was too bright, but that wasn't what was keeping Charlie awake. Everything was strange: the smell of the bedding, the hard mattress, the way the bunk squeaked whenever she moved. Charlie listened to the steady breathing of the others, and to the rushing sound of the sea. Even those sounds were strange. Very strange.

'Can't you sleep either?' came Hannah's voice. She looked different without her glasses.

Charlie shook her head. 'You want to come up?' she asked. 'It's a great view.'

'Ooh, yes please!' Hannah felt around for her glasses, then she sneaked past the sleeping Xa and clumsily climbed up on to Charlie's bed. Charlie thought she looked funny in her pink pyjamas.

'You've got a cuddly toy?' whispered Hannah.

'Of course!' Charlie gently tickled her chicken's neck. 'I couldn't bear to be parted from her. My mum gave her to me for my tenth birthday.'

'I brought mine as well,' said Hannah. 'But I didn't dare unpack it. I thought everyone would make fun of me.'

'Why? Izzie's got one,' replied Charlie. 'And Xa has one of her little brother's jumpers under her pillow.'

'Really?'

'Absolutely.' Charlie pulled the duvet up over her knees.

'But my teddy wouldn't help anyway.' Hannah sighed. She wrapped her arms around her knees and looked out of the window. 'I just can't sleep. Can't get my head to be quiet.'

'Why?' asked Charlie. 'What are you thinking about?'

Hannah brushed a strand of hair off her face. 'My parents are getting divorced.'

'Oh!' said Charlie. She'd had no idea. How awful for Hannah! Then Charlie realised it could never happen to her. Her father wasn't even around.

'They argue every day,' Hannah told her. 'And sometimes even at night. They argue about everything, and then my dad comes in and yells at me that I eat too much and says what do I think I look like anyway? And so my mum screams at my dad again, and then they send me to my aunt's for a few days, so they can carry on arguing on their own.'

'Sounds horrible!' mumbled Charlie. She didn't know what else to say.

'How does it feel?' Hannah looked at Charlie anxiously. Her glasses were all steamed up. 'I mean, only having a mother. What's it like?'

'Fine.' Charlie shrugged. 'It's fine with just my mum around. Only thing is she has to work so much. But, you know, that's just the way it is.'

'Hmm.' Hannah looked at her toes.

She sounded so sad. Charlie really wanted to comfort her, but she couldn't think how. So they just sat there in silence, side by side on Charlie's bed, and looked at the sea, which had been painted silver by the moon.

They sat like that for quite a while.

Then Hannah got cold and slipped back into her own bed. But not before she had fetched her teddy from her bag. It was a white bear, and it wore pink pyjamas just like Hannah.

## Chapter Seven

The next morning everybody seemed a little bleary-eyed. The weak, milky tea they had at breakfast did nothing to wake them up either, and when Mr Dudman announced they were going on a nice long walk to the next village, the temperature of the mood dropped below freezing.

'What's with the long faces?' he asked. 'We'll even be passing two very interesting prehistoric burial mounds.'

'Oh, I can't wait!' groaned Freddie. 'Two humps in the ground. Very exciting.'

'Unfortunately Mrs Rose won't be coming with us,' said Mr Dudman, ignoring Freddie's comment. 'She's feeling a little indisposed this morning.'

'I'm feeling indisposed, too!' Tom called out. 'Can I stay here as well?'

Mr Dudman ignored him.

Freddie was right about the burial mounds. No skeletons, no mummies, no treasure – just two humps in the ground. Mr Dudman joked that a tribe of trolls lived in the mounds, but if they did, they were nowhere to be seen. Instead, the boys got on everyone's nerves with their new water pistols, which could hold an annoyingly large amount of water. Only when Max drenched Mr Dudman were they all ordered to empty their weapons. And when it started to rain as well, the mood in the class turned mutinous. Even Helena had lost her usual cheerful good humour.

'So what do you think of these houses?' asked Mr Dudman when they finally reached the small village they'd be heading for. Thatched cottages sat under yew trees, all lined up in a row.

'Nice,' mumbled Hannah.

'They're all right, I suppose,' said Helena, fidgeting. 'Is there anything else to do here?'

'Well, not much, but we *are* here for a reason.' Mr Dudman put on his you'll-see-soon-enough face, the one he always used when he was returning homework.

'What reason?' shouted out one of the class.

Mr Dudman shook his head. 'One of you might be able to guess, but the rest of you will have to remain in suspense. Follow me, ladies and gentlemen.'

Grumbling, the class fell in behind him.

'What's that supposed to mean: "one of us might be able to guess"?' said Izzie, and Helena shrugged.

'Actually, the houses are really pretty,' said Xa. 'I like the wooden beams. And the gardens have so many flowers!'

'They're not like my gran's, are they?' Charlie linked arms with Xa. 'Are you still upset about yesterday?'

Xa shook her head.

'Then . . .' Charlie rubbed her nose, '. . . I mean, do you think you could let me have the baby monitor again?'

Xa pulled away her arm away like she'd been burnt. 'You're unbelievable!' she shouted. 'Completely unbelievable!'

'We can always switch it off, whenever . . .' Charlie started to stutter, '. . . I mean, *if* there's something about, you know . . . stuff.'

Xa walked off, furious.

'Oh dear!' muttered Charlie.

She watched as Tom picked a flower that was hanging over one of the fences. What a drip, she thought, watching him running after Xa.

'Xa's not going to let us have it, is she?' asked Helena catching up with Charlie.

'Are you spying on me now as well?' Charlie barked at her.

'No!' replied Helena, stung. 'It's not my fault you talk so loudly!'

Charlie's face darkened. She chewed her lip.

The street with the old houses led them to the harbour, where some boats were bobbing about while screeching gulls swooped down on the dark water. Mr Dudman led the class past some souvenir shops and stopped in front of a café.

'Right. Ladies? Gentlemen?' he called. 'Now it's time to reveal the true purpose of this dreaded outing. Amy, would you please come here?'

Amy turned as red as a tomato. Hesitantly she went to stand by the teacher's side.

'It's Amy's birthday today!' announced Mr Dudman. 'And my guess is, knowing you lot, nobody knew that. I think having a birthday calls for a celebration. So that is why I am inviting you all to join me in this café. For a hot chocolate, or a Coke, whatever you like, in Amy's honour. I, for one, will be having a large cappuccino.'

While Mr Dudman gave his speech, Amy looked down at her hands, smiling shyly.

Once they were inside, they pushed three big tables together. Mr Dudman sat with Amy at the top. He made the whole class sing 'Happy Birthday' – which he thankfully only conducted – before he ordered a round of drinks: ten hot chocolates and seventeen Cokes. Then he slurped his coffee happily and read his newspaper.

For a while, the boys were happy flicking paper

pellets across the table and bombarding the girls with sugar cubes. Then, bored, they all clustered around the only slot machine by the entrance to the café. Helena, the tireless spy, skulked nearby as inconspicuously as possible, while Xa bought Amy a piece of chocolate cake. Xa had Tom's flower tucked behind her ear.

Soon only Charlie, Hannah and Izzie were left at Mr Dudman's table. Hannah couldn't stop yawning, Charlie mulled over what she could put in the Piranhas' beds, while Izzie painted her nails. Suddenly Mr Dudman peered out from behind his newspaper.

'By the way, did anyone notice anything strange last night?' he asked. 'I'm not talking about your usual fun and games. Anything out of the ordinary? Inexplicable noises, maybe a scratching at the door? Unexplained lights on the beach? No?'

Charlie looked at him in surprise. 'Why?'

'Oh, nothing.' Mr Dudman reached for his coffee cup. 'I just wondered. You know how you – er – kind of hear about things sometimes.'

'What things?' Hannah stopped yawning for a moment.

'Oh, nothing special. Just something about the ghost of a long-dead coastguard.' Mr Dudman looked at them over the rim of his cup. 'He's supposed to haunt the beach right by our hostel. 'Course, it's all rather far-fetched, don't you think?'

'A ghost?' shrieked Helena excitedly, who'd over-heard the conversation. 'A real ghost? You're kidding!'

Even the boys at the slot machine turned around.

'Shh!' hissed Charlie. 'That lot don't need to know about it!' She turned back to Mr Dudman. 'What kind of a ghost?'

'Oh, for goodness' sake, there's no such things as ghosts,' said Izzie, going back to blowing on her freshly painted nails.

'I'm sure you're right, Izzie. But a colleague told me this story, and he swore blind it was true.' Mr Dudman cleared his throat. 'He came here last year with his class. And he said some really odd things happened . . .'

'What things?' breathed Hannah.

Mr Dudman shrugged. 'Spooky sounds in the night. There were strange footprints and mysterious objects found on the beach. Two children ran screaming from their room one night, jabbering about some horrible thing that had tried to drag them into the sea. I don't really know any more than that.' He tugged on his ear-lobe. 'But why am I telling you all this? You've got enough to do feuding with the Piranhas.'

'Those idiots?' Charlie waved a hand dismissively. 'We stopped all that childish stuff long ago, but they started it again. No, tell us more about the ghost! What did you say he was again?'

'A coastguard,' said Mr Dudman continuing. 'A

coastguard looks after the coast and those who sail near it.' He signalled to the waitress to bring him another coffee.

'If a ship sank near St Peter's Island, it was the coast-guard's job to make sure that the cargo stayed safe from looters. But they say that this particular coastguard was fond of a bit of looting himself. His name was Ben Penmarric and he's been haunting this island for more than two hundred years. The people here,' Mr Dudman stirred his coffee, 'still tell stories about his crimes.'

'What did he do?' whispered Helena, who had crept over to the table and sat down, her eyes wide.

Mr Dudman shook his head. 'I'm not sure I should tell you. He did some terrible things.'

'We're not babies!' cried Izzie indignantly.

'No, that's true, I suppose. Well . . .' Mr Dudman stopped and took a long-drawn-out slurp of his coffee.

'Well what?' asked Charlie, impatiently. Mr Dudman could be really annoying sometimes.

'OK, I'll tell you all I know,' he said, carefully dab-bing his mouth with his napkin. 'But if it gives you nightmares, don't say I didn't warn you.'

Chapter
Eight

'Ben Penmarric was a strange sort of coastguard,' began Mr Dudman. 'If a poor farmer stole a washed-up butter barrel because his children were starving, he'd have him flogged and thrown into jail. And he never raised a finger to help the crew of a stricken ship. Instead he just let them drown slowly, so there'd be no witnesses when he filched the cargo.'

'How awful!' muttered Helena. 'Someone like that was bound to end up as a ghost.'

'Is that so?' Mr Dudman looked amused. 'But that's not all. There was nothing that unusual in Penmarric not saving the drowning men. In those days nobody was inclined to risk their life for strangers. They might even steal some loot, too, but Ben Penmarric was a real blackheart and he went much further than that.'

Mr Dudman cleared his throat dramatically. 'Whenever there was a storm out at sea, he'd order his men to light fires along the clifftops, luring the ships on to the rocks below, where they'd be wrecked. The men would then steal the cargo as it washed ashore. And anybody on board who didn't drown in the icy waves was killed, so there was no one left alive to tell of what had happened.' Mr Dudman leant back and folded his arms. 'Let's just hope that his ghost is nicer than he was, right?'

'Was he never caught?' asked Izzie.

Mr Dudman shook his head. 'He was far too cunning for that.' He brushed some fluff from his jumper. 'Look out for Ben Penmarric's picture in the island museum when we visit this afternoon. And he's buried in the old cemetery, which we'll also visit at some point.' Mr Dudman lowered his voice. 'They say his gravestone stands crooked because Penmarric can never rest easy.'

'Ugh!' shuddered Helena. 'That's really creepy.'

'He just got away with it?' exclaimed Charlie, outraged.

'I bet he got filthy rich and then just died peacefully of old age,' said Izzie. 'Is that what happened?'

'Not quite,' answered Mr Dudman. 'You could say he met some kind of justice. Shortly before his fifty-fifth birthday, he was poisoned by the widow of a captain whose ship sank because of his rogue signals.'

'No!' Hannah's eyes were huge. 'How horrible!'

'Why? Serves him right!' said Izzie with satisfaction. 'I would have done the same.' She carefully painted a second layer of varnish on to her nails.

'That was a fantastic story!' exclaimed Charlie, her eyes shining. 'It's just such a pity that ghosts don't exist.'

Just then Tom sat down at the table, making them jump. 'What are you lot all huddled up for?' he asked nosily.

'None of your business!' replied Charlie. 'You just go back to your slot machine.'

'I'm sorry that you didn't hear anything last night,' continued Mr Dudman. 'And that you haven't found anything interesting. No old coins, I don't suppose? Penmarric is said to drop them when he's out haunting at night.'

The girls shook their heads.

'What are you talking about?' asked Tom. 'What strange noises? Who's Penmarric? What haunting?'

Oh no. Charlie clenched her fists. Now the Piranhas would know.

'Oh, we were just chatting about our hostel's resident ghost.' Mr Dudman picked up his newspaper. 'I wondered if anyone had heard anything strange between, say, ten and eleven o'clock last night. But it seems the ghost has gone on a holiday of its own.'

'A ghost? Excellent!' Tom was fidgeting with excitement. 'Tell me everything!'

'Find out for yourself!' hissed Charlie.

'All right, I will,' Tom shot back. 'You can bet on that.'

'Now, now!' said Mr Dudman, retreating behind his newspaper again. 'There's no need to be so unpleasant, Thomas. I'll tell you all about it on our way back.'

'Excellent!' Tom jumped up. 'I have to tell the others about this. This is much more exciting than thatched cottages and stupid mounds.'

He rushed back to the others and soon the Piranhas were whispering in the farthest corner of the café. They didn't even notice when Helena sat herself quietly down at the next table.

'Do you think the story is true?' whispered Hannah. 'I've always wanted to see a ghost. Maybe not one that nasty, though.'

'It's harmless,' said Izzie, 'because there are no such things as ghosts.'

Hannah chewed her fingernails. 'I'm not so sure about that.'

'Only because you watch silly movies,' teased Izzie. She looked over at the boys.

'No, it can't be a ghost, Izzie's right. But maybe . . .' Charlie rubbed her nose, like she always did when she was thinking, '. . . maybe someone is pretending to haunt the hostel to hide a secret: maybe they've buried something nearby and they don't want anyone nosing around on the beach.'

'Like what?' asked Hannah breathlessly.

Charlie drew a finger across her throat.

Hannah's face turned white. 'Oh no! A murder? That's horrible.'

'Stop it, Charlie!' said Izzie. 'You know what I think? If someone's pretending there's a ghost, then it's simply a story to attract visitors' attention.'

'Really?' said Hannah. 'That would be so disappointing. Maybe it's aliens?' Hannah lowered her voice. 'They do exist, you know. My father saw a UFO once.'

'Now there's another fascinating subject,' said Mr Dudman, folding up his newspaper. 'But it'll have to keep for another time, I'm afraid.' He glanced at his watch. 'We have to get back at the double, or we'll miss lunch.'

Chapter
Nine

They nearly did miss lunch, despite Mr Dudman setting a murderous pace. Worse, Hannah, Izzie, and Charlie had wanted to keep the ghostly goings-on to themselves, but not only did Mr Dudman tell the Piranhas all about Ben Penmarric, but he also made the whole class sing old sea shanties all the way back. It was awful.

Hoarse and out of breath, they all piled into the dining room and sat down wherever they could find empty places. Charlie, Izzie and Hannah sat at one table, with Xa still glaring at Charlie and sitting down with Amy at another.

Helena rushed over to the three C.H.I.X. and squeezed on to their table. 'I've got something to tell you!' she panted. 'I heard something. Two somethings, in fact!'

'Two what?' asked Charlie.

'Secrets!' hissed Helena.

Charlie looked around quickly, but the Piranhas were on the table farthest away, arguing about football with the other boys. Soon it turned into a mashed-potato fight led by Will, until Mr Dudman intervened. Charlie turned back to Helena with a sigh.

'OK, go on then.'

'The Piranhas are planning to catch the ghost!' hissed Helena.

Charlie frowned. 'Really? How?'

Helena shrugged apologetically. 'I don't know any more than that. They're going to come up with a plan tonight.'

'Typical!' said Charlie. 'And we don't have the baby monitor. Xa won't give it back. Just because that idiot Tom has gone all soppy over her.'

'Oh, who cares?' said Izzie. 'Even they can't catch a ghost that doesn't exist. They might as well try to catch the Loch Ness monster. Yum, this cabbage isn't half bad,' she said, rolling her eyes.

'What was the second secret?' Charlie asked Helena, looking round at the boys again.

'They've put something on our pillows,' whispered Helena. 'During breakfast, when Olly and Will pretended to go to the bathroom. They said we'd all think we had fleas! Olly got it in some shop where he buys his magic stuff.'

'Itching powder! They've put itching powder on our stuff!' Izzie shuddered. 'Oh, that's really bad. They know that Hannah is allergic to a ton of things.'

'I'm itching just thinking about it!' whispered Hannah.

'They'll pay for this!' hissed Charlie. 'After all, pillows can be swapped, right?'

Hannah and Izzie nudged each other and giggled.

'Helena,' Izzie said, hugging her, 'I think you'd be great in our gang.'

'Thanks!' Helena smiled gratefully. She looked at Charlie, who was pretending to be busy with her food.

'Charlie?' Hannah leant over the table. 'What do you say? Shouldn't we let Helena swear the C.H.I.X. oath? Tonight. As a reward, I mean!'

But Charlie frowned. 'This is all a bit quick, isn't it?'

'Nonsense!' Izzie pushed her empty plate to one side and tucking into her dessert. Hannah looked on longingly. 'Why make Helena wait? I say she becomes one of us tonight!'

'I agree!' said Hannah. She looked over to where Xa was sitting. 'And I'm sure Xa would too.'

Izzie grinned triumphantly at Charlie. 'You're outnumbered!'

'But what about our name?' Charlie pointed out.

'It's made up of all our initials.'

Silence fell, then Izzie began to grin. 'Just as well she's called Helena, then, isn't it?' she said. 'The "H" can stand for two C.H.I.X.'

Charlie opened her mouth to say something, then closed it again. 'Fine!' she grumbled. 'Whatever. I suppose it *is* thanks to Helena that we won't have to scratch ourselves to death all night. Having a spy turned out to be a not-half-bad idea.'

'What was a not-half-bad idea?' Freddie suddenly popped up behind Charlie and rested his chin on her shoulder. Charlie shoved him away.

'Get lost, football-for-brains!'

'Hey!' announced Olly coming over to where the girls sat. 'I've just had a GREAT idea. We should have a little bet – a *spooky* little bet.' His voice squeaked with excitement. 'Bet you we can catch the ghost and you can't!'

'Oh, the *ghost*.' Charlie pulled a face. 'Go ahead. We're old enough not to believe in ghosts, you know.'

'Duh! How stupid do you think we are?' said Freddie, scornfully. 'We don't believe in ghosts either! We're just betting you that we'll find out what's behind that ghost story before you do. But you know what I think?' Freddie leant towards Charlie until his nose was nearly touching hers. 'You're just too scared to accept the challenge.'

'That's a stupid bet!' said Izzie. 'What's there to find out? It's just a story.'

But Charlie stared thoughtfully at Freddie. She chewed her lip before finally saying: 'You're on. We bet you whatever you like.'

'We get a dance with the C.H.I.X. of our choice at the disco on the last night,' suggested Tom.

Will didn't look very enthusiastic, but Freddie and Olly grinned.

'Good idea, Tom!' said Freddie. 'So? Do we have a deal?'

Charlie shrugged. 'If that's what you want. Since we're going to win anyway—'

'And if we win,' interrupted Helena, 'you have to carry our bags for the whole trip back.'

'Done.' Freddie nodded. 'But since when were you part of the C.H.I.X.?'

Helena bit her lip. The C.H.I.X.'s spy had blown her own cover.

'She isn't,' said Charlie. 'But her idea's a good one. The bet's on.'

The C.H.I.X. and the Piranhas shook hands.

'Hey what about Xa?' asked Tom. 'Isn't she in the gang any more, or something?'

'Of course she is!' Charlie shot him her most withering look. After all, it was his stupid fault that she'd fallen out with her best friend. 'She'll be in on the bet.'

'Sure?' Tom looked over at Xa.

'Sure,' sighed Charlie.

Now she just had to convince Xa.

Chapter
Ten

**H**elena came panting up the stairs. 'The Piranhas are playing table football again!' She really was a first-rate spy. 'They've got a whole tournament going with Felix, Josh and the twins.'

'Are all of them playing?' asked Charlie.

'Well, it's two against two but they keep taking turns.' Helena grinned. 'They're so into it.'

Charlie gave a satisfied nod. 'Then let's go.'

The girls dashed up to their room. Ellie was downstairs, writing postcards, but Xa was there, sitting by the window and looking out at the sea. When the others came charging in she turned round, startled. 'What's up?'

'The Piranhas have put itching powder on our pillows,' said Hannah. 'So we're going to swap our pillows with theirs.'

'Itching powder?' Xa wrinkled her nose. 'Yuck!'

Charlie tried a cautious smile. 'Will you help us?'

Xa hesitated briefly. Then she shrugged. 'OK.'

Carefully the C.H.I.X. picked up their pillows and carried them to the door. Helena held it open for the others, then quickly followed them with her own pillow. They made quite a procession.

'And what do we have here?' Mr Dudman was standing by the hall window.

'We, erm . . .' For the life of her Charlie couldn't think of a good excuse.

'Never mind.' Mr Dudman turned back to the window. 'Forget I asked.'

The five girls exchanged relieved looks and quickly moved on.

There was a clumsy drawing of a skull and cross-bones stuck to the door of the Piranhas' room.

'Is that supposed to make us run for our lives?' asked Izzie.

Charlie put her ear against the door. 'Yeah. That skull isn't half as scary as your green fingernails.'

'Ha, ha!' Izzie stuck her tongue out at Charlie.

'Can you hear anything?' whispered Hannah.

'Nope. But wait a minute!' Charlie bent down. 'Check this out. They're not as stupid as they look. We should do something like this too.'

'What is it?' The others peered over her shoulder.

'They stuck a piece of paper across the door down here,' said Charlie, carefully removing the sticky note. 'If we'd just opened it and walked in, the paper would have been torn off and they'd have known someone had been in their room. But because they're dumb boys, they made it too obvious. I spotted it when I was listening.'

She balanced her pillow on one hand, opened the door with the other, and slipped inside. The others followed. They swapped the pillows as quickly as they could.

Charlie looked around. 'I don't believe it. They've even put up football posters.'

'And a huge flag.' Helena went to examine it more closely. 'What country has a flag like this?'

'It's just some football club's.' Izzie screwed her face up. 'How ridiculous.'

'Well, you've got posters of whatshisname on your wall,' said Xa. 'It's kind of the same, isn't it?'

Hannah giggled. 'His mouth is all smudgy from where she's been kissing it.'

'Shut up!' Izzie hissed at her. Her face had gone all red and blotchy.

'Right!' Charlie tiptoed back to the door. 'Let's get out of here.'

They scurried back into the corridor with the

swapped pillows. Charlie carefully replaced the sticky piece of paper, then they marched back to their room. Mr Dudman shook his head as he watched them go.

## Chapter Eleven

At least they didn't have to walk to the museum that afternoon. Dark clouds had appeared during lunch and it started raining as soon as they left the hostel. The grey sky hung low over the whole island.

'So annoying.' Izzie sighed. 'We probably won't even get to swim once!'

'Suits me,' said Charlie. She didn't particularly like the water. Most of all she hated getting ducked, which was probably one of the Piranhas' specialities.

The first thing they saw as they stepped off the bus was a huge arch made from the jawbones of a whale. It was a memorial to the time when a whale had got washed up on the shore. Through the white bones they could see the thatched barn that housed the museum.

'Eeew!' yelped Tom as he stood between the

bleached pillars of the strange arch. 'I really don't like walking under the bones of a dead fish.'

'Whales aren't fish,' said Helena, shoving him along.

A small round man with mutton-chop whiskers and tweed jacket was waiting for them by the entrance. He watched the unruly group approach with obvious disapproval.

'Could I have some quiet, please?' called out Mrs Rose. 'This is Mr Appleby, who has kindly agreed to give us a tour of the museum. Now, there are a few rules. No touching the exhibits,' – at this Mr Appleby nodded his head vigorously – 'don't knock anything over, and, above all, pay attention.'

'Listen to that last rule in particular,' added Mr Dudman, raising his voice, 'because once we get back to school, you will have the pleasure of writing an essay about what you have seen.'

There was general moaning and groaning from the class.

Mr Appleby smiled nervously.

Although it was a museum, there wasn't much to see: century-old village photographs, nets, sea-maps, stuffed sea birds, and even a peeling lifeboat. Izzie spent a lot of time looking at what the villagers were wearing in the photos, while Olly got caught sniggering at a wooden figurehead of a naked woman. Mr Appleby was furious.

The last room was filled with portraits of local dignitaries . . . and Ben Penmarric, the evil coastguard from Mr Dudman's story.

'That's him!' Helena whispered to Charlie. 'Did you imagine he looked like that?'

'No!' Charlie shook her head. 'He looks so harmless. Maybe he wouldn't have made such a good ghost after all.'

The C.H.I.X. and the Piranhas scrambled over each other to get as close as possible to the painting.

'He doesn't look like a murderer at all,' muttered Xa. The others had filled her on on Mr Dudman's story and all about the bet with the Piranhas. She was embarrassed by the last bit.

'No, indeed, Ben Penmarric didn't look like a criminal at all,' joined in Mr Appleby. 'Which was why he managed to lead a double life for so long – as a wrecker and as a pillar of the island's community.'

'Is it true that he haunts the island now?' called out Freddie.

Mr Appleby exchanged an amused glance with Mr Dudman. 'That's what people say.'

'Weird!' whispered Olly. He looked closely at Ben Penmarric's clear blue eyes.

'So what does he do?' asked Will. 'I mean, when he's out haunting.'

'Well, the story goes that he wails and scratches at

walls,' Pleased, Mr Appleby looked at the class, who were suddenly quiet and attentive. Rarely did he get such a rapt audience! 'He's also said to leave wet, sandy footprints from wandering the beach where he killed all those poor sailors. People have claimed to find old coins in the sand, as if by leaving them, Ben Penmarric was trying to pay for his sins.' Mr Appleby rocked back and forth on his feet, enjoying himself. 'That's what the legend tells us, anyway. The legend,' he turned to face the gloomy portrait of the coastguard, 'of Ben Penmarric, the most terrible wrecker St Peter's Island has ever known. And there have been many!' Mr Appleby looked at the children crowding around him. 'Any questions?'

'Is there a painting of the woman?' asked Izzie. 'The one who poisoned him?'

Mr Appleby shook his head regretfully. 'Sadly not. But we do know a few things about her. Her name, for example, was Margaret Mullholland, and she wouldn't have had the money for a portrait. That was quite a luxury in those days.'

'Shame, I would have liked to have seen her,' whispered Hannah.

'What happened to her?' asked Charlie.

'What do you think?' Tom grabbed his own throat. 'Urgh, hanged.'

'Oh, no, that's not it at all.' Mr Appleby shook his head. 'After doing the deed, she disappeared with her four children. Some fishermen probably took her to the mainland. Some say half the island helped her escape.'

'How romantic!' Helena sighed.

'Hardly,' said Mr Appleby. 'The rest of her life would have been far from romantic. She was a widow with four children. She had no money, no property, no family. It would definitely not have been romantic.' Mr Appleby glanced at Mr Dudman. 'But I think that's enough about her.'

They returned to the hostel in time for dinner. Afterwards, even though it was already dark, Charlie managed to persuade Mr Dudman to go with them to the beach. While he sat in the dunes, the C.H.I.X. scoured the sand with their torches, looking for Ben Penmarric's coins for a laugh. And of course, the Piranhas soon turned up. Freddie had wangled a shovel from the hostel's caretaker, and set to searching for buried treasure like a human bulldozer.

Charlie eyed the boys suspiciously. 'At least Freddie and Will are on punishment kitchen duty tomorrow, so they can't find out too much.'

'I *really* hope they don't find anything,' breathed Helena.

So far the girls had only turned up a few crabs, seashells and a couple of empty beer cans.

'Hey!' called out Hannah suddenly. 'I've got something! It's a coin. There!'

The Piranhas stopped digging and stared over at the C.H.I.X.

Izzie pointed her torch at Hannah's find. 'That's just an old 10p piece,' she said.

The Piranhas hooted with laughter and went back to work, taunting the girls for ages after that. But they didn't find anything either. After an hour the girls lost interest. They were frozen stiff and their clothes were damp from the sea air. Even their lips tasted salty. The boys had also abandoned their search and were huddling together on the sand. The C.H.I.X. flopped down and looked gloomily out to sea. Only Xa remained cheerful.

'I could sit here for ever,' she murmured. 'It's so beautiful. If you close your eyes, the sound of the waves goes right through you.'

Hannah shut her eyes tightly. 'You're right,' she said. 'I can feel it way down in my belly.'

'Well, my bum's frozen stiff,' said Izzie. 'I'm going back. Why were we doing this anyway?'

Mr Dudman came striding over from the dunes. 'Had enough for one day?' he asked.

'Yes.' Charlie scrambled to her feet. 'It was a dumb idea digging in the dark.'

'Wait!' shouted Hannah. 'What's that?' She scrabbled in the sand, not far from Mr Dudman's shoes.

'What, there?' Izzie sighed. 'Not another 10p piece?

Come on, let's go inside. I need a cup of hot chocolate.'

'No, look!' said Hannah scooping something up. 'Here. These are quite old.'

Curious, the others leant over her sandy hand. The Piranhas jumped up and came closer. Hannah had found three large, rusty coins. 'Look, Mr Dudman,' said Xa.

Mr Dudman took the coins from Hannah and studied them closely. 'Yes, coins like these have not been in use for a long time,' he confirmed. 'You never know, this could indeed be some of Ben Penmarric's blood money.'

He put the coins back in Hannah's hand, and she closed her fingers tightly around her find.

'Hey, Hannah,' said Freddie. 'You'd better lock your door tonight. Everybody knows ghosts always come to get their money back.'

'They *always* do!' shouted Tom. 'Not that locking the door will do you any good. Old Ben can just stick his bony hand through the wall next to your bed.'

'Shut up!' shouted Charlie. 'You're just jealous because you didn't find anything.'

Hannah shoved her hand with the coins into her pocket, chewing her lip anxiously.

'Come on, Hannah.' Charlie pulled her along. 'Ignore them. They're such idiots.'

The C.H.I.X. followed Mr Dudman through the

dunes. The bright windows of the hostel were a welcome sight after the darkness of the beach.

'Whooooooo!' The Piranhas howled behind them. 'Aaaaaargh! Tonight Old Ben's coming for scaredy-cat little fat Hannah!'

'You're so mean, you bullies!' shouted Helena, throwing handfuls of wet sand at the boys.

'Just ignore them!' Charlie whispered to Hannah. 'They're just jealous.'

'Exactly!' Izzie linked arms with Hannah. 'And remember,' she lowered her voice so that Mr Dudman couldn't hear them, 'they'll soon be scratching themselves silly, and then they won't be able to think about anything else.'

'I don't care what they say!' said Hannah, even though she was trying not to cry. 'But since none of you believe in ghosts and stuff, I'd really like one of you to take the coins.'

The other C.H.I.X. looked at each other. None of them reached out to take the coins from Hannah.

'Oh, give them to me!' said Xa, finally. 'I'm only afraid of real-life criminals. And Ben Penmarric is as dead as a dodo.'

## Chapter Twelve

After they had brushed their teeth, the C.H.I.X. locked their door. Charlie even wedged a chair under the handle. Ellie lay on her bed making fun of them, but the C.H.I.X. ignored her. They had more important things to do, like getting ready for Helena's swearing-in as their newest member. In celebration, Izzie decided that the room needed dressing up, so she hung her pink silk scarf in front of the window. She even tried to put a bow on Charlie's cuddly toy, although Charlie soon put a stop to that. Xa made some rose leaf tea, and Hannah lit some candles they had brought with them. Helena fetched the mugs. She was so excited that she dropped one, but luckily it didn't break.

'Do you think the Piranhas have already gone to

bed? I wonder if they're feeling itchy yet!' asked Charlie.

'They're probably waiting for us to turn in,' said Izzie. 'Which means they've got a long wait ahead of them.'

They all sat around the table.

'Could we turn off the light for a bit, Ellie?' asked Xa.

'Whatever for?' she replied.

'To make things more fun!' answered Hannah. 'Helena will be swearing the C.H.I.X. oath in a minute.'

A loud groan came from Ellie's bed. 'Oh! You're such a bunch of babies!' she said. 'All right, but just for five minutes and not a second more.'

The big, bare room immediately looked much cosier in the candlelight.

'Right!' said Charlie. 'Helena, do you still want to be in the C.H.I.X.?'

Helena's eyes were huge. 'Oh yes!' she breathed. 'More than anything!'

'Then stand up and repeat after me . . .'

Helena jumped to her feet so quickly she nearly spilled her tea.

'I swear . . .' began Charlie.

'I swear . . .' repeated Helena.

'. . . to guard the secrets of the C.H.I.X. . . .' Izzie continued.

'. . . to guard the secrets of the C.H.I.X. . . .' said Helena.

Hannah took over: '. . . with my life, and never to tell anyone anything.'

Helena repeated: '. . . with my life, and never to tell anyone anything.'

'Or I will drop dead on the spot,' finished Xa.

Helena swallowed hard. 'Or I will, erm, drop dead on the spot.'

Ellie chuckled. She thought all this was hilarious. 'What *are* you on about?' she asked.

'Oh, shut up!' said Charlie, angrily. 'Spit on your palms, everyone. You too, Helena.'

The five girls spat on their hands, then they clapped them together.

'Done!' said Charlie. 'Now we are five.'

'There's strength in numbers!' Izzie carefully wiped her fingers with a tissue. 'Five against four. Those Piranhas won't know what's hit them!' She gave Helena a nudge. 'How do you feel? Now that you're a real member of the gang?'

'Wonderful,' whispered Helena.

'Now all you need is a chicken feather,' said Xa. 'Charlie can get you one from her gran's chicken coop.'

'That won't happen any time soon,' grumbled Charlie. 'My gran and my mum aren't speaking –

again. You'll have to make do with your gull's feather for now.'

'Lights on!' shouted Ellie. 'I want to read! Ugh, why am I so itchy all of a sudden? Have you had a cat in here? I'm allergic to cats!'

'Oh, no!' giggled Hannah. 'You know what? We forgot to swap her pillow!'

'Oops!' Xa and Izzie were giggling, too. They couldn't help themselves.

'What do you mean?' roared Ellie. 'You forgot to swap my pillow? Forgot to swap my pillow with what?'

'The Piranhas had put itching powder on the pillows,' explained Charlie, grinning broadly as she switched the lights on. 'So we swapped ours with the ones from their room. But we forgot to take yours.'

'Itching powder?' Ellie was frantically scratching her head and neck. 'I don't believe it. I really don't believe this!' She jumped out of her bed and ran to the little sink in the corner.

'What does itching powder feel like?' asked Helena. 'Is it . . . really itchy?'

Ellie gave her a murderous look. 'Now I'll have to wash my hair as well,' she muttered. 'Just because of you and your silly jokes.'

'I can lend you some good shampoo!' said Izzie, with an angelic smile.

Ellie didn't even look at her.

'I wonder the boys are doing.' Charlie stood listening at the door. 'I can't hear anything. Great! We can have another look at Hannah's coins, then.'

'There they are.' Xa put them on the table.

Hannah eyed them with finder's pride – and with a little unease too. 'They look really old.'

'So? That doesn't mean Penmarric dropped them. I still think this is all a tourist gimmick,' said Izzie.

'Even so, I'm going to sit by the window tonight and keep an eye on the beach,' said Charlie. She walked to the door. 'But first, I'm going to check on the Piranhas. Don't want to miss them all scratching themselves like a bunch of monkeys with fleas. I'd never forgive myself.' She pushed the chair aside and unlocked the door. 'Anyone coming?'

'Me!' said Helena.

Ellie was wrapping a towel around her wet head. 'I hope they catch you,' she hissed.

Hannah grabbed Charlie's sleeve. 'Can't you stay here? I mean, because of the ghost and all that.'

'Don't be daft!' Charlie slipped through the door with Helena in tow. 'It's much too early for ghosts. Lock the door behind us and don't let anyone in. Understood?'

'Understood!' said Izzie, closing the door behind them.

The corridor was pitch dark. Only tiny slivers of

light came from under the doors. Charlie and Helena could hear laughter from some of the rooms, and in one somebody was bouncing on a squeaky bed. Mrs Rose's room was silent, but there was a thin band of dim light coming from under her door. Mr Dudman's room was in darkness.

'Should we turn on the hall light?' whispered Helena.

'Why not? We could just say we needed the loo.' Charlie flipped the switch, but nothing happened.

'That's weird,' she muttered. 'Did you bring your torch?'

'No, I forgot,' whispered Helena.

'Never mind,' Charlie whispered back. 'Let's go.'

She carefully tiptoed up the corridor. She could hear loud splashing from the boys' bathroom. And swearing. Angry swearing. It was the Piranhas!

'Listen to that!' giggled Charlie. 'The boys are taking showers. Their joke backfired spectacularly on them. Another victory for the C.H.I.X.!'

'That's what you think!' someone growled behind her.

Helena uttered a little shriek. Charlie spun around in surprise. Someone grabbed her and covered her mouth. She knew that grip; it could only be Will. Meanwhile, Freddie had Helena in an arm lock.

'Will and I had a little pillow fight,' said Freddie. 'Which is probably why we're not scratching . . .'

Charlie glared at him. She couldn't say a thing, because of Will's hand over her mouth. She tried to bite it, but not even that made him let go.

Helena looked miserably at her. Charlie tried to stamp on Will's feet, but she couldn't reach them. Will had had too much practice to fall for that one.

'Let's go, Willster – to their room,' whispered Freddie. 'But watch out – Rosey isn't far from them. Have you got our little gift?'

Will nodded.

Ah yes, Mrs Rose. Charlie had just been about to reach for Will's hair. But then she remembered that if they got caught fighting then they'd all be in trouble. Big trouble. Mrs Rose did not like gangs at all.

And so Charlie let herself be dragged to the C.H.I.X.'s room. Helena wriggled and kicked, but Freddie did not let go of her.

'Hey, you in there!' He knocked on the door three times. 'Open up!'

For a few moments there was silence. Then they heard rustling behind the door.

'No way!' answered Izzie.

'Er, yes way!' said Freddie quietly.

'We have Charlie and Helena!' Will hissed through the keyhole. 'And we'll tickle them until you open up.'

That did it for Charlie. Never mind Mrs Rose. She would not be held hostage. Ever.

She yanked one arm free of Will's grip, grabbed a handful of his hair, and pulled it with all her might. Backwards. Will squealed like a pig. For one startled second he loosened his grip, and that was all Charlie needed. As quick as a flash she freed herself. An angry Will was not good to be around, and angry didn't come close to describing him at that moment. His face was a picture as he tried to grab Charlie, but she ducked out of his reach and jumped on Freddie to try to help Helena.

At that very moment the girls' door opened.

Charlie couldn't believe it.

Ellie was standing in the doorway, her towel still wrapped around her head. 'I've had it up to here with you lot!' she screeched. 'Stop all this right now!'

Red in the face, Izzie pushed in front of her. 'We didn't want to open the door,' she panted. 'But *she* was too quick.' Izzie shot Freddie an angry glance. 'Let go of them. You won't get in here, not even with the help of your little friend!'

Ellie stuck her tongue out at Izzie.

Freddie grinned. 'We don't want to come in,' he said. 'We just want to give you something to remember us by.'

Will pulled something from his pocket and threw it to Freddie, who threw it over Ellie's head into the room.

Charlie knew immediately what it was.

And to make the whole disaster complete, Mrs Rose was now coming down the corridor. 'You lot!' she shouted. 'I might've known! And there was me thinking you'd buried the hatchet. What . . . ?' Mrs Rose sniffed and her face screwed up with disgust. 'A stink bomb? Have you gone mad? You do know that we could be thrown out of here for this? Have you even read the house rules?'

'It was just a joke!'mumbled Freddie. He didn't even dare look at Mrs Rose.

'A joke?' she said sharply. 'Maybe I should have a little joke and call your parents. Hmm? Who threw that thing?'

The C.H.I.X. and the Piranhas stayed silent, as was the unwritten rule. But they had forgotten about Ellie. No rules for her.

'Him!' she said, pointing at Freddie. 'He threw it. And now I have to sleep with this smell.' Her voice was trembling with rage. 'I don't even have anything to do with their stupid gang stuff.'

'You can sleep in my room,' said Mrs Rose. 'As for you . . .' She shook her head as she looked at the C.H.I.X. 'I'm inclined to believe you brought this on yourselves. Still, the stink bomb was thrown by the boys, and so they should suffer the consequences. My suggestion is you all swap rooms for the night.'

The C.H.I.X. looked far from delighted.

'It's all right, Mrs Rose,' said Charlie, quickly. 'We want to stay in our room. We can handle a bit of stink.'

'I wouldn't get a wink of sleep in their room,' added Helena.

'Oh?' Mrs Rose gave her a surprised look. 'Are you part of this silly gang now, Helena?'

Helena looked at the floor.

Mrs Rose sighed. 'You heard them,' she said to the Piranhas. 'But I promise you, if there is even the tiniest bit of monkey business at night from now on, I will split you up and put you each in a different room. Understood?'

'Yes, Mrs Rose!' groaned the C.H.I.X. and the Piranhas.

Mrs Rose looked up at the light fitting. 'Is the lack of light out here also your doing?'

'We unscrewed the lightbulb,' admitted Freddie.

'Then I suggest you give it to me right away,' said Mrs Rose. 'And I repeat: this is the last time anything like this happens. Is that clear? Otherwise this trip will be over for you. You can mess around outside during the day. No matter what happens, I will not expect to see your faces out here again after nine.'

'And what if the ghost comes?' asked Freddie. 'How are we going to track it down if we can't even leave our room?'

'Oh, old Penmarric!' Mrs Rose shook her head. 'I can see that story has made an impression on you. If that old blackguard turns up, you can always call me or Mr Dudman. But I think it's highly unlikely, don't you? Now off to bed with you all.'

Freddie prodded Will to turn around.

'This time you went too far!' Charlie hissed at them.

'OK, OK, don't go on about it!' grumbled Freddie.

And then he and Will slunk off back to their room.

**X**a scrubbed the floor where the bomb had hit until her back ached. They opened the window as wide as it would go. But the awful smell just hung around, as if it had sunk into the very walls. The room got really, really cold, and soon staying up was just not possible any more.

The five girls tucked themselves into their beds, duvets pulled right up to their noses. But sleep wasn't possible either, the boys had seen to that.

Apart from the sound of waves breaking gently on the shore outside, there was silence. No more giggles from the neighbouring rooms.

'Well, we completely ruined this evening,' said Xa, her voice sounding loud in the quiet. 'If we keep it up, we might even spoil the whole trip.'

'We?' said Charlie hugging her cuddly chicken tight, although it didn't make her feel any warmer. '*They* brought the itching powder, *and* the stink bomb.'

'I know.' Xa sighed. 'But we should stop it now. They've had their fun, and we've had ours, so let's just call it quits. We only have three days left here. Or shall we carry on and ruin them too?' She paused for a moment. 'Tom says he doesn't really like all the fighting either.'

'Oh, that's it!' said Izzie. She pushed her duvet off and climbed out of bed. 'I've had enough, and I'm closing the window!'

'Can you see anything out there?' asked Hannah.

'Old Penmarric, you mean?' Shivering, Izzie leant out of the window. 'Oh yes, there he is, floating about down there, wailing. Eew, gross! He's all mouldy, and the skeletons of his victims are dancing around him.'

Hannah looked at her suspiciously.

'Eeeugh! I can't watch!' Izzie held her hand over her eyes. 'Now he's pulling their bones apart and throwing them into the sea.'

'Ha! Very funny!' muttered Hannah. But she still climbed out of her bed and tiptoed to peer over Izzie's shoulder.

'I knew it,' she said almost disappointedly. 'Nothing. Absolutely nothing.'

'Exactly!' Izzie patted her cheek. 'Not that you could

see anything anyway without your glasses.' She slammed the window shut and turned around. Suddenly she stopped short and looked Hannah up and down.

'Oh no! Where did you get those pyjamas?'

'My mum got them for me. Why?' Hannah looked down at herself. 'She buys all my things.'

'But you look like a big baby!' said Izzie. 'What was she doing, buying you something like that?'

Without a word, Hannah turned around and crept back into bed, pulling the duvet up to her chin.

'Iz! Do you have to be so horrible?' asked Charlie. 'We don't say anything about *your* stupid clothes.'

'So?' Izzie spun around to face her. 'What should I say? Wow, Hannah, what great pyjamas. I wish I had some like that?'

They could hear Hannah sobbing now.

'You could try saying nothing for once,' said Xa.

'Like *you* do, you mean?' Izzie's face had gone red and blotchy. 'You all know I'm right, but you never say anything. You think that helps Hannah?' Izzie crouched down by Hannah's bed. 'Look, I'm sorry about the pyjamas, but tomorrow I'll do your hair. I know how to do it. My cousin showed me. She's a real hairdresser. And your mum can't do a thing about it. What do you reckon?'

'What will you do to my hair?' Hannah peered over

her duvet. 'I'm not sure . . .'

And that's when they all heard it.

Horrible, howling laughter in the corridor.

The five girls exchanged startled looks.

Then something scratched at the door.

Charlie shot out of her bed. She reached for the door handle.

'No!' squeaked Helena. 'Leave it!'

But Charlie had already poked her head out of the door. In a flash all the other C.H.I.X. were behind her.

'What can you see?' asked Xa.

The light was switched on and there was a face peering round every door along the corridor.

'What was that?' asked Bella. Bella did karate, and she was definitely not afraid of ghosts.

'Was it a cat?' called Lily, from the girls' room next door. Their door was only open a crack.

Mr Dudman was also there. He was standing in his doorway in a bright yellow dressing gown, his hair all dishevelled. 'Interesting,' he said. 'I'm obviously not the only one who heard strange noises. Was that what woke you, Mrs Rose?'

Mrs Rose had come tottering sleepily out of her room. She looked totally different without her eyeliner and red lipstick. 'A very unpleasant laugh,' she said. 'That's what woke me. And then something scratched on my door. Poor Ellie dived under her bed. Tell me honestly, you lot . . .' She looked sternly at the Piranhas and the C.H.I.X. 'Was that you again?'

'No!' replied both gangs, indignantly.

'It seems that, for once, they had nothing to do with this,' said Mr Dudman. 'I was already out here when I heard that last scratching sound.' He shrugged. 'The corridor was brightly lit, but there was nothing to be seen. Absolutely nothing. The doors were all shut and all the rooms were relatively quiet. It's all rather strange, I must say.'

'The evil coastguard!' whimpered Helena.

'Told you so!' Freddie called out. 'He wants his money back. Hannah should have left those coins on the beach.'

'Some ghost!' muttered Tom. 'Turning up at eleven. If it'd been midnight, we'd have been ready.'

'Ready for what?' asked Mr Dudman.

'Nothing, just stuff that needed doing,' said Freddie, quickly. He shoved Tom back into their room.

'Olly, what have you been up to?' asked Mrs Rose. 'Spit it out!'

Olly wriggled like an eel, but Mrs Rose's hawk-like gaze was worse than the threat of Freddie's sharp elbows.

'We've got some banana skins,' he muttered, 'erm . . . to make the ghost, or whoever, slip up.'

The C.H.I.X. exploded with laughter.

'Banana skins!' Charlie taunted them. 'Of course! You guys are priceless!'

'Do you have anything else?' asked Mr Dudman.

Olly shrugged. 'Only a bucket of water . . . and we put a bit of ink in our water pistols.'

By now the whole class was sniggering.

'Olly!' groaned Will.

'You will stop all that immediately!' said Mrs Rose. 'Before you decide to use them on the C.H.I.X. instead. And as far as that laughing, scratching ghost is concerned,' – she looked directly at each and every one of them – 'if I catch him, his haunting days will be well and truly over.'

She yawned as she turned back to her room. 'I can get very grumpy,' she called over her shoulder, 'if I don't get my sleep.'

With that Mrs Rose slammed her door shut. For the last time that night.

## Chapter Fourteen

**O**nce again, Mr Dudman's whistle kicked off the day.

The C.H.I.X. groaned and pulled the duvets over their heads. On the fourth whistle Charlie finally crawled out of her bed. Despite the cold, she had spent half the night sitting by the window, while the others were peacefully sleeping. But there hadn't even been the palest shadow of a ghost to be seen.

The room was still very smelly.

Charlie stumbled to the window and looked outside. Dark clouds hung over the sea. The sun poked through them every now and then, making the water glitter as if someone had poured silver over it. But the next moment the heavy clouds were back.

'No swimming today,' announced Charlie, 'but it's

the perfect weather to visit a graveyard.' She yawned as she shuffled to the little sink by the window, which got them out of a visit to the bathroom in the morning. That was one good thing about their six-bed room.

'Oh, I love graveyards!' Hannah pushed her duvet aside and put her glasses on. 'At home we sometimes go for walks in the cemetery, and read the inscriptions on the gravestones, or look at the angels. They have beautiful angels there.'

'I know! Bet you have to be really rich to get one of those,' said Izzie. She sat on the edge of her bed and started brushing her hair, just as she always did first thing each morning. 'We'll probably just get a plain stone with nothing on it apart from our names.'

'Speak for yourself!' said Charlie. She had finished washing and made way at the sink for Xa. 'Mine is going to say: "Here lies Charlotte. She had some really good ideas."'

'Ha ha!' giggled Hannah.

In the corridor, doors were beginning to be slammed. People were running around and somewhere they could hear Mr Dudman giving orders.

'I think graveyards are sad,' said Helena. 'I'd rather have my ashes scattered over the sea. I even put that in my will.'

'Will?' said Xa, waking up as she brushed her teeth. She could never get a word out before she'd cleaned them. 'You've made a will? Already?'

'Of course,' said Helena. She climbed into her jeans, ran her fingers through her hair and rummaged in her bag for her warmest jumper. 'You never know. My aunt died when she was twenty-one. That's not that old, right? I wrote down who gets my guinea pig so that it won't end up abandoned. My books and my games will go to my brother. And then I also wrote down that I'd like my ashes to be scattered over the sea.'

Hannah looked at her, speechless.

Izzie shrugged. 'That's not such a daft idea. I might do the same.' She looked in her bag. 'What does someone wear to a graveyard?'

Charlie and Xa rolled their eyes and grinned at each other.

At that moment the door opened and Ellie came in, looking glum.

'I need my toothbrush,' she said, not looking at any of them. 'And some clean underwear. Yuk!' She held her nose. 'It still smells like a sewer in here.'

Charlie looked at her icily. 'And whose fault is that?'

'Oh, leave her alone!' Xa nudged Charlie out of the way and went over to Ellie. 'We're sorry we forgot to swap your pillow. We didn't do it on purpose. Honestly!'

Typical! Charlie rolled her eyes. Xa just couldn't stand anyone being angry with her, or things being unfair. And Xa saw lots of things that she thought were unfair. Far more than Charlie ever did.

Ellie looked at Xa in surprise.

'That's OK,' she said finally. 'And about the stink bomb . . .' She fiddled uneasily with her toothbrush. 'I'm sorry about that. I had no idea those idiots would do something like that.'

'Oh, the Piranhas love that kind of stuff,' said Izzie. 'Stink bombs, itching powder . . .'

'. . . slime, plastic spiders, fake puke,' added Hannah. 'Olly gets it all for them when he buys his magic supplies. It's his true passion.'

'You must never ever shake hands with him,' warned Izzie. 'He sometimes puts this sticky stuff on his hand. It takes ages to wash off.'

'Thanks for the warning.' Ellie chose some clean underwear and two new magazines from her rucksack. She hesitated, then she turned around. 'I'm going for a shower,' she said over her shoulder. 'See you later.'

'See you!' Xa called after her.

Once Ellie had gone the C.H.I.X. looked at each other.

'She's not so bad, is she?' said Helena quietly.

'Nope.' Xa shook her head. 'And definitely no worse than us.'

At least they got a break from the Piranhas that morning. Freddie and Will were doing kitchen duty, while

Olly sat at the breakfast table shuffling his cards. Tom was probably off somewhere composing another note to Xa.

It didn't last, though. In the bus on the way to the cemetery, the boys teased the girls about the stink bomb. Fortunately, Mrs Rose dampened their mood by confiscating their water pistols.

The cemetery lay behind an old brick church between two nearby villages, and was surrounded by high trees. They took a quick look inside the church, decided it was boring, and filed out into the graveyard. There were really old graves, and much more recent ones, all divided by small hedges and neatly cut grass. This time they didn't have a Mr Appleby to guide them, but Mrs Rose had brought a little book about the graveyard with her. She led the class along narrow paths to the older part of the cemetery. Some of the graves there were nearly two hundred years old. All the gravestones were inscribed with strange, swirly lettering and decorations of ships, anchors, or twining foliage.

'There are flowers on this one,' said Tom.

They were standing by a gravestone showing a ship dwarfed by huge waves. Beneath the ship a list of names had been chiselled into the stone, together with a long indecipherable text.

'What does it say, Mrs Rose?' asked Hannah. 'Can you read it?'

Mrs Rose shook her head. 'But there might be some information in my handy little book. Hang on . . . yes, this is the grave of a sea captain,' she said. 'His name was Bill Fredericks. He married four times, surviving all his wives, who gave him seven children – but only two survived – and he died at the age of ninety-one,' Mrs Rose read out loud.

'I wouldn't like to have a life like that,' said Izzie. 'Sounds awful. Nearly everyone died before he did. His wives, his children.' She shook her head. 'Nah! Not even the longest life can make up for that. I bet his wives died quite young, too,' she observed, while Hannah thoughtfully stroked the wings of one of the stone angels.

'The children often died when they were really little,' murmured Xa. 'Sad, isn't it?'

'So where's the grave of Ben Penmarric?' interrupted Will. 'That's what we're really here for, isn't it?'

'Not entirely,' said Mr Dudman. 'But we could have a look around. His gravestone will be all crooked, remember?'

They spread out and started looking for a wonky stone. Suddenly someone cried out: 'There! In between those two crosses. That's a *really* crooked one.'

The Piranhas rushed over while the C.H.I.X. deliberately followed at a more leisurely pace. 'There's his name!' Olly traced it with a grubby forefinger.

'So it is!' Mr Dudman leant forward. 'There he is. Ben Penmarric. Born October 23rd 1740, and, as it says here poetically, "sank into death's arms" on September 14th 1795.'

'Two hundred years ago tomorrow,' said Xa.

'Exactly!' breathed Helena. 'What do you think that means?'

'It doesn't mean anything!' Mrs Rose shook her head. 'You really are a superstitious bunch.'

'Could you read what else it says?' Hannah's eyes were wide with anticipation.

'There's not as much as on the other gravestones,' said Mrs Rose. 'Ben Penmarric was a successful merchant who was married twice and was blessed with a son.'

'That's it?' The Piranhas stared incredulously at Mrs Rose.

'What about all the sailors he murdered?' cried Charlie.

'None of that would have been put on his gravestone,' said Mr Dudman. 'Ben Penmarric's son would have paid for it. He wouldn't have wanted to be remembered as the son of a murderer! No. He must have hoped that in time his father's crimes would have been forgotten. But . . .' Mr Dudman paused for effect, '. . . that was not to be. Stories would have been told on long winter nights, and soon enough everybody would have known the truth.'

Mrs Rose shivered suddenly. 'I think I've had enough dark tales for one day.' She looked at the sky. The sun was breaking through the clouds. Mrs Rose held up her face to the warming rays. 'What do you think?' She looked at the children. 'Shall we get out of here?'

Nobody seemed keen to stay a moment longer.

As they all crowded on to the bus, Tom pushed his way over to Xa and slipped another note into her hand. He hoped that nobody would see, but Charlie saw, and smiled ruefully.

Izzie had won her bet.

Chapter
Fifteen

Lunch was great — spaghetti and tomato sauce with three meatballs for each of them! While they enjoyed their pasta, Charlie wondered if she should ask Xa about the note. But she didn't dare.

Xa noticed that her friend kept looking at her. She smiled, and gave Charlie one of her meatballs. That was Xa all over! She was far too good for the likes of Tom. But Charlie still didn't ask her about the note. The baby monitor had taught her a lesson about being nosy.

While Freddie and Will took the plates back to the kitchen after dessert, Mrs Rose told Hannah that there was a phone call for her. The other C.H.I.X. waited until all the tables had been cleared, but Hannah didn't come back.

'Maybe she's gone to the loo?' suggested Izzie.

Xa shook her head. 'I don't think so. It must be something to do with that call.'

'Perhaps she just went up to the room?' said Helena hopefully. 'Do you think?'

'Come on!' Charlie jumped up. 'Let's find out.'

Mr Dudman and Mrs Rose were walking down the stairs as the girls rushed out of the dining room.

'Do you know who called for Hannah?' Izzie asked Mrs Rose.

Surprised, Mrs Rose looked at her. 'Her mother. Why?' She looked around. 'Where is she, anyway?'

'Oh, she's probably upstairs,' said Izzie.

They quickly ran up the last steps and along the corridor.

Hannah *was* in the room.

She was lying on her bed, staring at the wall.

'Hannah?' Charlie went over and sat down next to her. 'What's the matter?'

Hannah sniffed. 'Nothing!' she said, her voice wavering. But she didn't turn around.

'Would you like to be left alone?' asked Xa anxiously.

Hannah nodded.

Charlie got up again. 'Are you sure?' she asked quietly.

At first Hannah did not move, but then she shook her head and started to cry. Loudly. It was a terrible sound.

'Hey, hey!' Izzie sat on the edge of her bed and stroked her shoulder. 'What is it? Tell us. You can talk to us.'

Finally Hannah turned around. Her eyes were all puffy.

'Has something happened?' asked Helena, concerned.

Hannah nodded. 'My dad moved out,' she mumbled. 'Yesterday.' She rubbed her eyes, which were all red with crying.

'Oh no! Couldn't your mum have waited till after the trip to tell you?' murmured Izzie. 'She must've known how it'd make you feel. Look, give me your glasses. They're all steamed up.'

Hannah took off her glasses and gave them to Izzie. 'She said terrible things about him,' she sobbed. 'And that he should never come home again.'

Izzie gently rubbed Hannah's glasses on her skirt and put them back on her friend's nose. 'Never mind!' she said. 'He only ever gave you a hard time anyway.'

'Still!' Hannah started sobbing again.

Xa sat down on the bed and gave her a hug.

'Shall I make some tea?' Charlie said, feeling a bit out of her depth.

'Yes, please!' Hannah managed a smile, but it was a very watery, wobbly one. 'Does anyone have a hanky?'

'I do!' Helena quickly produced a large, crumpled

one from her pocket. 'Here. It's clean. Just looks dirty, that's all.'

'Thanks!' For a few moments Hannah's face disappeared into the handkerchief while she blew her nose. 'I don't want to go home again,' she said hoarsely. 'I have no idea what I'm supposed to do there. I wish we could all stay here together for ever.'

'But we're together when we're at home, too,' Xa pointed out. 'And you know, as soon as we get back, we have to do a lot of stuff to our C.H.I.X. hang-out, to get it ready for winter.'

'Right.' Hannah blew her nose again.

'There.' Charlie put a mug of hot tea into her hand. 'I put honey in it.'

Hannah gratefully sipped the hot, sweet tea.

'Anyone else want a cup?' asked Charlie.

'Well, if you're offering!' came a loud voice. 'Milk and two sugars, darlin'!'

It was Tom and Olly.

Of course, they *would* have to turn up at that very moment. They were leaning against the open doorway, grinning. Distracted by everything that was happening, none of the girls had heard the door being opened. Hannah hid her puffy face in Xa's jumper.

'Olly's got a new trick and he needs a glamorous assistant to cut in half!' yelled Tom. 'Any volunteers? Or are you all just too ugly?'

Olly giggled like a small boy.

'Oh, leave us alone, you idiots,' said Izzie.

'Yes, go play with your silly football table!' added Helena.

'Football table!' Tom shook with laughter. 'It's called table football, stupid. And anyway, why are you hanging around with this lot? You're not one of the C.H.I.X.'

'I am now!' said Helena, proudly.

'What?' Tom fell against the door frame with a groan. 'Did you hear that, Olly? There's five of them now.'

He sneaked a quick glance at Xa, but she wasn't paying any attention. She was busy comforting Hannah.

'Can't you see you're intruding?' Charlie shouted at them. 'Just go away, will you!'

'What's happened?' asked Olly.

'None of your business,' spat Charlie. 'And next time knock, OK?'

'Like you do, you mean?' Tom looked at Xa again, but she just frowned at him.

'You really are intruding,' she said. 'OK?'

'All right, all right, we get the message.' Tom turned around huffily. 'Come on, Olly. We've got some ghost-hunting to do.'

Charlie slammed the door shut behind them.

'And you're happy to get love notes from *him*!' she said to Xa. 'I can't believe it. He's the biggest idiot of them all.'

'Stop it!' shouted Hannah. 'Don't you two start fighting as well!'

Charlie bit her lip. 'Sorry!' she mumbled. 'It just kind of slipped out.'

'I think you should apologise to Xa,' said Izzie.

'Sorry!' Charlie mumbled again. But she couldn't meet Xa's eye.

'It's not my fault that he writes me love notes!' cried Xa. 'And he's not always like that. That's just when he's with his stupid gang.'

Charlie just looked into her mug. Her tea had gone cold.

'Pssst! Charlie, Xa, Helena!' hissed Izzie, waving them over to the window while Hannah washed her face at the sink. 'I think Hannah needs a distraction,' she whispered. 'And I have a BRILLIANT idea . . .'

Chapter
Sixteen

**C**harlie knocked on the boys' door. They were all inside. Tom opened the door to her and Izzie.

'Hey, Freddie!' he called. 'Look who's here.'

Freddie and Will were sprawling on their beds. They looked at the girls in surprise.

'What's this?' asked Freddie, groggily. 'You challenging us to a duel?'

'Charlie and I have a proposal,' said Izzie.

Freddie jumped out of his bed, and immediately realised that he was only wearing boxer shorts. His face went bright red as he quickly climbed into his jeans and patted down his ruffled hair. He went over to the girls.

'Right, we're listening,' he said.

'It doesn't look like it,' observed Charlie. Tom and Olly were nudging each other, whispering and sniggering.

'Oi! You two!' Freddie barked at them. 'Shut up for a second, will you?'

'We're proposing a truce,' continued Izzie. 'Twenty-four hours. Maybe even longer.'

'Why?' sneered Will. 'Are you scared that Rosey will split you up and put you in different rooms?'

'Of course not!' Charlie hissed at him. 'Hannah's parents are getting divorced, and she's really upset about it. We thought we'd have a picnic on the beach, take her mind off things a little. And your stupid itching-powder-stink-bomb attacks are the last thing we need. That's why we want a truce. What do you say?'

'Fine by me!' said Tom. 'We haven't got any more stuff anyway, right, Olly? Our magical genius only bought one stink bomb.'

Freddie looked at him crossly. 'Just shut it, all right?' He turned to the girls. 'OK, truce agreed. But what about the ghost?'

'There's always tomorrow to go ghost-hunting,' replied Charlie. 'Right now, Hannah is more important.'

Freddie turned to the others. 'What do you think?'

'Old Ben isn't going anywhere,' chirped Olly. 'And if Hannah needs cheering up, I can always do some tricks for her.'

'I'll let her know,' said Charlie, turning away, but Freddie grabbed her arm.

'Hold on,' he said. 'Now that we have a truce . . . we

found something weird the other day.' He went to the wardrobe and got out . . . Xa's baby monitor.

'Did you lose this, by any chance?' asked Freddie.

Charlie tried hard to avoid Freddie's eye. 'Possibly,' she mumbled. 'Let me just take it back and check.'

'At first we thought it was some kind of charger,' said Olly. 'But then Tom recognised it. His parents have one for his little sister.'

'Really?' Charlie looked at Tom and bit her lip. Was the truce over already? What if they went to Mrs Rose? The C.H.I.X. would be dead! But Freddie just broke into a smile.

'I hope you heard some juicy stuff,' he said, chucking the monitor to Charlie. She gave a huge sigh of relief. 'Got to hand it to you, sometimes you're quite clever, you C.H.I.X. Shame we didn't think of this.'

'Yeah, who knows what we might have heard!' sighed Tom.

'Yeah, bad luck,' shrugged Charlie. 'But you had some pretty cool ideas, too.'

Truce in place, Izzie and Charlie returned the baby monitor to Xa – undamaged, and without any ransom demands. The Piranhas could be all right sometimes – for boys.

The picnic turned out to be a brilliant idea.

Of course, they weren't allowed to go to the beach by

themselves. Mrs Rose positioned herself at a discreet distance with her book. Mr Dudman stayed in his room, 'to recuperate', as he put it. No one had any idea what he meant by that.

There was hardly a cloud in the sky, but the wind was still blowing quite strongly off the sea. The girls' bags of crisps were blown away twice, but both times Helena sprinted after them and retrieved them just before they ended up in the Piranhas' mighty sand castle. The boys were building this with great gusto, having spent an hour having a laugh looking for Penmarric's blood money. They found instead a few shreds of cloth, which Freddie swore were from his death shroud. He put them on display on the top of their castle, framed by seashells and pebbles, as if they were the crowning glory or something. Fluttering above everything was their favourite football flag, on a broomstick that Freddie had 'borrowed' from the kitchen.

'It's amazing!' Helena looked jealously at the boys' masterpiece. 'Why don't we build something like that?'

''Cos it's too much like hard work!' said Izzie, letting herself flop on to her back on the sand. 'Right now I don't want to do anything. No walking on the beach, no museum, no graveyard, no digging up ghost-coins, nothing!' She squinted into the sun. 'Just look at that blue sky. It's endless.' She sighed again as she folded her hands behind her head. 'Could someone pass me the crisps?'

'This picnic's brilliant,' said Hannah. 'It feels so good just to sit here.' She looked at the sea. 'Just imagine living right by the sea. Must be fantastic, don't you think?'

'I don't know.' Charlie took a handful of the soft sand and let it run through her fingers. 'I think all that wind and the waves would drive me crazy.'

'How could that be possible?' giggled Izzie. 'You're already nuts.'

'Oh yeah?' Charlie chucked a load of sand on to her friend's stomach.

'Yuck!' Izzie jumped to her feet and danced about to try and shake the sand from her clothes. The Piranhas whooped and cheered enthusiastically.

'Hannah?' asked Xa. 'Do you mind if I invite Amy over? I mean, it's your picnic . . .'

'Of course,' said Hannah. 'Bring her over.'

Xa immediately jumped up and tramped over the sand to where Amy was sitting on her own, watching some other kids from their class play with a ball. Happily, she followed Xa back to the picnic.

'Now all we need is for Ellie to join us,' mumbled Charlie.

'Ssh!' said Izzie.

'Hmph,' Charlie grumbled back.

Xa gently nudged Amy to sit down between Hannah and herself.

'Hello!' said Charlie, doing her best to look friendly.

'Hi,' mumbled Amy. She looked around the group of girls.

Izzie held out the crisps. 'Would you like some?' Amy reached gratefully into the bag.

'Hey!' exclaimed Helena. 'We nearly forgot Hannah's present!'

Hannah looked at her in surprise.

'Is it your birthday?' asked Amy. Hannah shook her head.

'It's not, but . . .' Charlie shrugged, '. . . we thought she could do with a bit of cheering up.'

'Why?' Amy gave Hannah a concerned look.

Hannah cleared her throat. 'My parents are getting divorced. This is a picnic to cheer me up, organised by my best friends. Oh no!' She brushed away a tear. 'Why do I always have to start crying?'

'There!' Helena put a little package in her lap. 'Now you can unwrap this.'

'I'd love to, but . . .' Hannah gave her glasses to Izzie. 'Could you clean these for me first?'

Izzie got to work, although it wasn't easy with her sandy skirt.

'My parents are divorced, too,' said Amy. 'They have

been for quite a while now.'

'Really?' Hannah turned to her with a smile of relief. She knew her friends were only being nice, but why did horrible things always seem to happen to her? It felt great to meet someone who was going through the same thing for a change.

Amy shrugged. 'Yeah. There's no fighting at home any more, but – you know.' She dug her bare toes into the sand.

'Here, Hannah, your glasses,' said Izzie.

'Thanks,' mumbled Hannah. She fumbled with the bow Helena had tied around her present. Finally she tore open the paper. Inside was a little box, decorated with tiny seashells.

'Oh!' Hannah gently lifted the box into the air and studied it carefully. 'It's beautiful. Thanks. What shall I put in it?'

'Penmarric's coins,' said Charlie.

'No!' Hannah shook her head. 'I wish I'd never found those things.'

Amy was looking puzzled, so Helena was quick to explain. 'Hannah found three old coins on the beach. We think it's blood money dropped by Ben Penmarric, the ghost. Did you hear him last night?'

'That creepy laugh?' Amy nodded. 'I thought it sounded like one of those giggle-box machines.'

The C.H.I.X. looked at each other.

'I didn't know you could buy anything like that,' said Izzie.

Charlie rubbed her nose.

'Look, Charlie's thinking!' said Izzie. 'Absolute silence, please.'

'Where are the coins now?' asked Charlie. 'Did anyone bring them?'

Xa shook her head. 'They're still where we left them on the table last night.'

Charlie jumped up without another word and dashed off. Helena immediately followed her, leaving the others looking after them in surprise.

## Chapter
## Seventeen

**G**asping for breath, Charlie and Helena arrived at their room.

'My trap,' panted Charlie. 'Look, the paper's been torn in half.'

A shred of paper was stuck to the door and another to the frame.

'Maybe whoever ripped it is still in there!' breathed Helena. Instinctively, she took two steps back.

'Only one way to find out . . .' Charlie pushed the door open.

No coins were on the table. No matter how hard they looked, on the floor, under the chairs, the money was gone. And there was water all over the floor.

'It's as if someone in big wellies walked through here,' whispered Helena.

'Wet footprints,' muttered Charlie. 'Didn't Mr Appleby say something about that at the museum? That the ghost leaves wet footprints?'

Helena looked at her wide-eyed.

'Yes, he did!' she said. 'You think it's . . . ?'

She looked around.

'Duh!' said Charlie impatiently. 'There's no ghost here. And there never has been a ghost here, either. Because ghosts don't exist. That's something Izzie and I actually agree on. No, I think someone is playing a huge trick on us. Question is – who?' Charlie looked at Helena. 'Did you notice if any of the Piranhas disappeared from the beach today?'

Helena shook her head. 'I don't think they did. They've been digging all afternoon. All of them. And then they just sat around their football flag, mucking about.'

'Hmm.' Charlie rubbed her nose. 'So they have alibis. And it's unlikely to be them, anyway. Too obvious. Hmm.' She was thinking so hard, she nearly chewed her lip off. 'No, there's someone else behind this.'

'But what if it *is* a ghost?' Helena looked anxiously at the wet patches.

'If there's a ghost hanging around in broad daylight,' said Charlie, 'then I'm a Piranha.' She dragged Helena out of the room and closed the door. 'Ghosts go through walls. This one,' she leant down and pulled off the torn piece of paper, 'came through the door. Like a human being.'

'But,' said Helena, 'the footprints . . . look! They stop at the door and don't go down the hall.' She lowered her voice. 'As if whoever made them just disappeared.'

'You're right.' Charlie stood up from where she'd been examining the prints and looked down the bone-dry corridor.

At that moment, Mr Dudman's door opened.

'Are the others still at the beach?' he asked briskly. 'It's almost time for us to go.'

Charlie sighed. They were meant to be visiting the ruins of some ancient defences, or something.

'Mr Dudman!' Helena leant in closer. 'Hannah's coins are gone. And our bedroom floor is covered in wet footprints.'

'Really?' Mr Dudman looked amazed. 'Maybe it was the old coastguard after all? Perhaps he'll put in an appearance later tonight during our ghost walk.'

'Ghost walk? What ghost walk?' gasped Helena.

'Who knows,' Mr Dustman walked with the girls to the stairs, 'maybe we'll finally come face to face with old Ben – or what's left of him.'

'What's left of him?' Helena was tugging anxiously

at her hair. 'You mean, he's no longer . . . no longer whole?'

Mr Dudman raised his eyebrows. 'I've no idea, Helena. I'm not an expert on ghosts, I'm afraid.' He looked at Charlie. 'So. Are you going to tell your rivals about this newest incident?'

'The Piranhas?' she replied. 'No, why?'

'Oh, no reason.' Mr Dudman looked around. 'I'd better try and find Mrs Rose. See you later.'

'Yeah, OK,' mumbled Charlie. She rubbed her nose again. Quite hard.

'Do we *have* to go on a creepy walk in the dark? Tonight of all nights?' asked Helena. 'I'm getting a bit scared. Aren't you, Charlie?'

Charlie shook her head.

'Do you think the ghost will show up?' asked Helena.

'No, I don't think so,' replied Charlie carefully. 'At least, not a real one. But I do think that *something's* going to happen, that's for sure.'

That didn't do much to calm Helena's nerves!

## Chapter Eighteen

The ancient defences proved to be as dull as expected. Mr Dudman did tell some impressive stories about Viking invaders, but they were all still glad when it was time to go back to the hostel. After dinner the Piranhas went to play table tennis. The C.H.I.X. decided to join them. Table tennis was the only sport Hannah liked, and they still had a lot of time to kill before the ghost walk. Time enough for Hannah to fall back into her gloomy thoughts. So they played table tennis for two hours, until they were hot and sweaty, and half their spending money had been swallowed by the drinks machine. It was great.

Helena sat by herself on the window ledge. She couldn't play table tennis. She got them drinks from the machine and kept asking what the time was. Izzie made a silent promise to teach her to play as soon as they got back home.

To Helena's great relief, the games room was locked at nine o'clock, just as the Piranhas had nudged into a nine-ten lead thanks to Olly's skill with the bat. Mrs Rose sent them all up to their rooms with the instruction to be back in the entrance hall at eleven. Warm clothes and working torches were obligatory.

'Eleven? Why eleven?' asked Helena in a slightly shaky voice. 'That means we'll still be out there at midnight.'

'Be afraid . . .' groaned Will, staggering towards Helena, his arms raised, 'be very afraid. I aaaam the ghoooost of Ben Penmarric!'

'Shut up!' Charlie shoved him angrily.

'Yeah. I'm not scared at all!' shouted Helena.

But she was. Everybody could see it. She was as white as a sheet, as if she were a ghost herself.

'Whatever . . . let's go!' Izzie pulled Helena with her up the stairs.

'But I am *not* scared!' squeaked Helena. 'Really, I'm not!'

'Everybody's a little scared of walking in the dark,' said Charlie, pushing Helena into their room.

'Exactly.' Izzie switched on the light. 'But that's the point. It's supposed to be creepy.'

Helena looked at her uneasily.

'I had to go out in the dark once,' Hannah told them. 'At summer camp. It was awful stumbling around, I was terrified.'

She sat on her bed and reached under her pillow to get the seashell box the others had given her. She carefully placed inside her treasures from the trip: a sachet of sugar from the café, her ticket from the museum and a pebble from the beach.

Izzie yawned as she changed out of her jumper and started rummaging through her bag. 'What am I going to wear?'

'Something white!' said Charlie. 'So we can all see each other.'

Ellie came in with two girls from the room next door. Over lunch the three of them had discovered a passion for the same music.

'Hi, Izzie,' one of them greeted her. 'Do you know what you're going to wear to the disco on the last night?'

'Absolutely,' answered Izzie. 'But it's a secret!'

The other girl just shrugged.

'Aargh,' groaned Charlie. 'Is that all you can think about?'

'*You* can talk!' said Ellie. 'I heard you and the Piranhas are off hunting a ghost with wet feet.' Her two new friends laughed so hard, they could barely manage to climb on to Ellie's bed.

'Well, you heard wrong then!' said Charlie through gritted teeth. 'We're hunting the person who's *pretending* to be the ghost.'

'Oh dear, that sounds way too complicated.' Ellie grabbed her earphones and joined the other two.

'Charlie,' whispered Hannah, 'what if there really is a ghost?'

'There are no ghosts!' said Izzie impatiently. 'You can bet your life on it.' She pulled a black knitted dress over her head.

'That's not white!' protested Charlie.

'I feel like wearing black,' replied Izzie. She began to brush her hair. 'And it's the warmest thing I've got.'

'Could you please listen to me?' begged Hannah, biting her lip. 'If it wasn't a ghost who stole the coins and left the prints, then it could have been someone even more dangerous? Like a real criminal!'

'Oh, no!' Helena pressed her hand to her mouth.

'For goodness sake! Why would a real criminal bother to steal a few old coins?' said Charlie. 'No, there's definitely something else behind all this.'

'Maybe those coins are incredibly valuable?' said Hannah. 'Like rare stamps or something.'

'Well, he's got them now, anyway,' observed Xa drily. 'So there'll be no more haunting and you can all stop driving yourselves crazy. Can't we just enjoy the walk? It's really lovely by the sea at night. It's so peaceful, and you can listen to your feet crunching in the sand and the rushing of the waves.' She sighed. 'Wonderful. I'd like to do it every night.'

'What a load of slushy nonsense!' scoffed Ellie from her bed.

Helena and Hannah just looked at Xa dumbfounded.

## Chapter Nineteen

**B**y the time they stepped outside, the wind had picked up quite a bit. The night was pitch black, as the moon was only managing to peek through the dark clouds. Giggling and shouting, the whole class followed Mr Dudman and Mrs Rose down to the beach. There was no chance of hearing anything over the racket they were making, let alone your footsteps in the sand, or even the sound of the waves. Poor Xa!

'Hey, girls!' called Freddie. When Charlie turned around she found herself looking straight into the beam of his torch. The Piranhas were trudging through the darkness right behind them. 'In this weather you really don't have to worry about ghosts. The wind would blow them away.'

The Piranhas kept up their laughter. Only Olly kept

looking around anxiously. Their torches barely made any difference in such darkness.

'Today,' boomed Tom in a deep, gravelly voice, 'is the anniversary of Ben Penmarric's death. It is time for him to find a new victim!'

'Stop it!' shouted Hannah over her shoulder. 'That's not funny.'

'Yes, leave it, Tom!' said Will. 'The g-g-girls are afraid of g-g-g-ghosts . . .'

'You could even say they were a bit chicken!' hooted Olly.

Charlie spun around. 'Is this you sticking to your side of the bargain?'

'What bargain?' asked Hannah.

'Never mind,' muttered Charlie.

'OK, OK,' said Freddie. 'We're only mucking about. We thought you liked our jokes!'

'And we were worried that you'd be afraid of the dark,' Tom added, grinning broadly.

Xa shot him a look that wiped the smirk off his face.

'Look, you idiots,' said Izzie. 'If I'm forced to go on a walk at this time of night, through darkness and wet sand, then I'd at least like to do it in peace, so I can look at the stars, or listen to the sea, and think about how I feel about stuff. OK? And I can't do any of that if you're behaving like stupid little boys.'

'Oh, Izzie!' Freddie dropped to his knees and

clutched his hands to where he thought his heart might be. 'We want to feel things too. Honest!'

'Yes, we love the stars and all that,' added Olly. 'We really do!'

Izzie shook her head, but she couldn't help giggling a little, much to Charlie's disgust. 'Come on,' she ordered. 'Let's not hang about with these idiots.'

'We get the message!' Freddie made a deep bow. 'Charlie doesn't want to star-gaze with us. We'd better leave them to it.'

'But don't think we'll come back and save you when the ghost turns up,' said Will.

With that the four boys sprinted past the straggling line of children and disappeared ahead into the darkness.

Izzie was still giggling. 'They're kind of funny, don't you think?' she said.

'Are you kidding?' growled Charlie.

'Oh, come on!' Xa gave her a gentle nudge. 'They were just having a laugh.'

Finally there was some peace. Most of the class walked in silence, or whispered quietly to one another. They pointed their torches at their feet, or at the sea, where the pale fingers of light were swallowed up by the dark waves. The C.H.I.X. also walked in silence. Charlie had linked arms with Xa; Izzie with Hannah and Helena. The night sky looked vast, and as the wind blew away more and more of the clouds, the darkness above them began to be dotted with stars. Mr Dudman even came walking down the line with a big plastic bag.

'I'm collecting torches,' he said.

'Why?' Hannah immediately hid hers behind her back.

'So that for once you get to enjoy the sky at night without artificial light,' answered Mr Dudman. 'At least that's what I'm telling you. I told the boys it was a test of courage. You pick the one you like best. And if anyone absolutely doesn't want to part with their torch,' he looked at Hannah, 'they can of course keep it.'

Hannah bit her lip. She looked at Izzie, and then at Charlie – and then she threw her torch into the bag with the others. She just clutched Izzie's arm a little tighter afterwards.

'Have fun!' said Mr Dudman. 'We're walking to that dune over there. You should be able to make it out, even without your torches. From there we'll be following the wooden walkway that'll take us straight back to the hostel. OK? I'll be bringing up the rear.'

With that he carried on walking to the back of the line.

Charlie turned around. Behind them were only Ellie and her two friends.

'Where's Amy?' Charlie asked Xa.

'She's up front, with Mrs Rose.' Xa lowered her voice. 'You know what? She and Hannah were talking all through dinner about divorce and their parents and everything. I think it's really good for Hannah to see that Amy has the same stuff to deal with.'

Charlie just said: 'Hmm.'

Lots of children in their class had parents who had split up. But Charlie was the only one who didn't even know who her father was. It was a weird feeling. But what good would thinking about it do?

'Charlie!' Helena suddenly whispered beside her.

'What?'

'Did you hear that?'

'What?' Charlie and Xa stopped and listened.

Helena was not the only one who'd heard something. The whole class had stopped and everyone was pricking up their ears.

'It's just the wind!' said Izzie.

'What kind of wind makes a noise like that?' Hannah's voice was trembling.

Then they all heard a howl, followed by a hollow moan. It came from across the beach.

They heard Olly yell, 'The ghost! Mrs Rose! There – it's the ghost!'

Charlie saw a few dark figures running towards the sound in pursuit. It looked like Freddie and Will. One of them still had a torch. Cheats!

'The noise is coming from up ahead!' Izzie called out. 'From that dune.'

Charlie ran. A couple of times she nearly stumbled over her own feet in the dark. But she just had to find out who was playing this prank on them all. And if Freddie dared to find out, then she did too. The wet sand sucked at her shoes, making running hard work. She noticed that the other C.H.I.X. were right behind her.

'Here!' shouted Helena. 'Charlie, I still have my torch!'

Relieved, Charlie grabbed it and pointed the beam of light towards the dune. The howling and moaning was getting louder and louder. Ahead there was nothing to be seen, except for the backs of the running Piranhas. Wait a minute! Mr Dudman was also sprinting towards the creepy noise. He was making better progress than the girls and soon he'd have caught up with the boys.

'Wow, who knew Dudman could run that fast?' panted Izzie.

Gasping for air, they struggled up the dune and stopped at the top. The Piranhas were standing along from them just a few metres away. The ghostly noises were coming from somewhere down below, from the darkness down between the dunes. Charlie and Freddie pointed their torches but their light fell on nothing but sand and long grass.

And still the howling grew louder.

'It's horrible!' said Hannah.

Helena looked at the others. 'I don't really want to go down there,' she said.

The Piranhas also seemed to be hesitating.

But Mr Dudman hadn't stopped. His overcoat flapping behind him, he was floundering down the sandy slope.

'What's he doing now?' Hannah was aghast.

'The ghost is going to get him!' whispered Helena. 'I saw something like that happen to someone on TV. That was quicksand, though.'

They all stared breathlessly into the dark hollow between the dunes.

'The moaning's stopped!' whispered Izzie suddenly. 'Listen! It's all quiet!'

The other four listened.

It was true. They could only hear the wind. The wind and the sea.

Then they heard Mrs Rose calling: 'What's going on up there?' She had stayed back with the rest of the class. Only four other children had joined the C.H.I.X. and the Piranhas on their chase.

'It's all right!' Mr Dudman called from below. 'There's nothing here, except for a few empty cigarette packets.'

*What?!* Without stopping to think, Charlie tucked Helena's torch into her pocket and slid down the dune to where Mr Dudman was standing. The other C.H.I.X. and the Piranhas followed.

At the bottom, they all looked around, mystified.

'Nothing!' said Freddie, angrily kicking the sand. 'There's absolutely nothing here. That can't be right.'

He looked at Charlie. 'Did you see anyone running away?'

Charlie shook her head.

'But we should've seen someone!' Tom sounded scared. Charlie had never heard him sound like that before.

'It's very strange indeed!' said Mr Dudman. 'If this spooky stuff is some kind of stunt to attract tourists, then we should at least have found some evidence of who is doing it.' He looked around, frowning. 'After all, we all heard those ghostly howls quite clearly, did-n't we?'

'We really did!' nodded Will. 'I got goosebumps. Then I thought Penmarric was going to grab me with his mouldy hands at any moment.'

The others said nothing.

'Maybe he just disappeared into the dune,' said Helena, in a trembling voice. 'Ghosts can do that kind of thing.'

'Nah!' Charlie shook her head determinedly. 'I bet you someone's sitting out there in the dark, laughing their head off at us.'

'You think?' Hannah moved closer to Charlie and grabbed her hand.

'It hurts me to say it, but I agree with Charlie,' said Freddie. 'We're being tricked. Big time.'

Izzie sighed. 'Well, at least nobody can say this was a boring trip!'

'Right!' laughed Olly nervously. 'We've had the full works.'

'Come on, you lot.' Mr Dudman started back up the dune. 'We should get back to the others. Or do you want to poke about in the dark a bit more?'

Xa shook her head. 'No. What's the point? If it was a ghost, then it's gone. And if it was a person then they won't be hanging around for us to find them.'

'Good point!' agreed Mr Dudman. 'For the time being we'll just have to accept the fact that we couldn't solve the mystery of the local ghost. Are you coming?'

That night Charlie didn't sleep a wink. She kept trying to find a connection between all the weird goings-on: the spooky laughter in the night, the stolen coins and the wet footprints that ended by the door to the corridor. And now the howling in the dunes.

Outside a sliver of dawn light was painting the sea red. Suddenly, Charlie had a thought. A crazy idea . . .

There was no way she could know that Freddie was having the same idea at exactly the same time.

Chapter
Twenty

The next morning the weather was perfect. On the last day of their visit, St Peter's Island was bathed in sunshine, and for the first time the sea was truly blue. Even Charlie felt the urge to wade into the waves. It was almost as if the island were trying to make it hard for them to say goodbye.

Hannah felt especially sad as she looked out of the window.

'It's so beautiful here,' she murmured. 'I can't bear to think that we'll be leaving tomorrow.'

'Don't think about it then!' Izzie put on her sunglasses. 'Easy!'

Hannah didn't think it was easy at all.

'Is your skirt in the Guinness Book of Records?' asked Charlie. 'As the shortest skirt anywhere ever?'

'Ha-ha!' Izzie adjusted her sunglasses. 'Not everyone likes running around in the same pair of jeans every day, you know.'

'Come on!' Xa pushed the two of them towards the door. 'Let's not start all that again. We're late for breakfast already.'

The only free table was the one next to the Piranhas. The boys all had glum faces, as though they'd been given pancakes for breakfast and then told they weren't allowed to eat them. They didn't even lift their heads when the girls sat down.

'What's got into them?' asked Xa.

'Good morning, everyone!' Mrs Rose got up and clapped her hands. 'Could I have some quiet, please?' She was wearing pink lipstick, as she always did when the weather was nice. 'Now we're all here,' she said, looking meaningfully at the C.H.I.X., 'I'd like to announce the plan for today.'

'Please!' Izzie raised her eyes to heaven. 'Not another walk!'

Mrs Rose continued: 'We were going to visit the seal sanctuary today. But I just discovered that it's closed due to illness. We've barely managed to touch on the subject of the environment on this trip. But,' she gave Mr Dudman a smile, 'we can always catch up on that back in class.'

'Why do we constantly have to listen to all that

green stuff?' muttered Freddie. 'I've never dunked a sea bird in oil. I recycle every piece of paper and every bit of glass, and what do my parents do? They just chuck it all in the rubbish anyway. Chuck, gone, off to be landfill.'

Mr Dudman grinned. 'Oh, I can see you're very well informed. I'm already looking forward to reading your essays.'

The faces of the Piranhas fell a little further.

'So back to the plan!' Mrs Rose tried again. 'I'll keep it short: there is no plan! We thought we might all benefit from a day to ourselves. This last day is all yours. There's only one rule: stay here at the beach. No one leaves without asking us first. And,' she lifted her hand, 'Mr Dudman and I would like to invite you to a beach barbecue this afternoon at three. And tonight, as I'm sure you've all remembered, we have our farewell disco from eight to ten.'

'Fantastic! No walking!' Izzie clapped her hands. 'And I will actually get to wear my new bikini! How about it, C.H.I.X.? Shall we see if Piranhas can swim?'

'Them? Get wet?' said Charlie. 'They already look like drowned rats.'

The Piranhas were flopping about on their chairs. Olly was half-heartedly performing some sort of trick, but it didn't seem to be lifting their mood.

'What's up with them?' Helena wondered.

Suddenly Izzie had a thought. 'Hold on. What day is it today?'

Xa looked at her in surprise. 'Saturday. Why?'

'Well, that's it, then!' She started to laugh. 'Oh, dear, the poor boys!'

'I don't get it,' said Charlie. 'What are you talking about?'

'Goes to show you really don't know boys at all!' Izzie leant over the table and lowered her voice. 'Saturday afternoons there's live football on telly. I sometimes watch it. It's quite exciting. I bet the boys never miss a game. And what don't we have on the island?'

'Telly,' said Hannah.

'Or phones, or iPods, or anything. At least, we're not meant to.' Charlie grinned. 'So *that's* why they're looking like that!'

Izzie nodded. 'I bet you anything. Wait, I'll prove it. Hey, Freddie!' She turned to the Piranhas. 'What are you doing this afternoon? Like, between half-three and half-five? Will you be watching the football? Oh!' Izzie put her hand over her mouth as if suddenly realising something. 'I'm sorry, you can't, can you? What a shame!'

Will looked at her as though he'd like to bite off her head.

'You're SO not funny, OK?' snapped Freddie. 'We'll

find a TV somewhere! This ban is completely stupid anyway.'

'Told you!' Izzie winked at Charlie.

'Mr Dudman's Mp3 player has a radio,' said Helena. 'Maybe he'll lend it to you?'

'We already asked him,' muttered Tom. 'That's not going to fly.'

'He said he hates football!' said Olly, outraged. 'And that he was not going to "aid and abet us in turning our brains to mush", whatever that means.'

'"Turning our brains to mush",' repeated Freddie. 'What a joke. I bet the thing's just gathering dust in his room – when he's not listening to the *news*, that is.'

'Maybe there's a radio in the common room,' suggested Hannah. 'There's always football on Saturday nights. I know because my dad . . .' She stopped and bit her lip. 'Because my dad always listens to it.'

'There you go then, boys.' Izzie got up and straightened her dress. 'I'm sure you'll survive.'

'Exactly,' added Charlie. 'Though why do you want to watch your team getting thrashed anyway?'

The boys howled with fury as the C.H.I.X. fled laughing from the room.

## Chapter Twenty-one

The Piranhas were barely seen all day. They spent a while making some modifications to their sand castle, but then they disappeared into the hostel again. Mrs Rose was sunbathing on her towel reading a crime novel, while Mr Dudman policed the shoreline, paddling in the cold water with his trousers rolled up, ignoring everything going on around him unless someone was about to be dunked fully clothed into the sea.

Their last afternoon on the island was really quiet. Izzie spent most of the time lying flat on her back in her bikini, moving only to touch up the polish on her toenails. Hannah, Amy and Xa collected seashells and pebbles. Helena read *Harry Potter* which made her chew her fingernails with excitement. And Charlie sat and buried her toes in the sand. Her socks were the only things she'd taken off on the beach. She was thinking about the ghost again.

Finally, after she had buried and unburied her feet at least a dozen times, she said: 'I think I know who it is.'

'Who what is?' mumbled Izzie without opening her eyes.

'The ghost.' Charlie squinted into the sun.

'Oh, OK, let me guess,' replied Izzie. 'It's . . . hmm . . . yes, it's Mr Appleby, the man from the museum. He gets so bored that he's started to do some haunting in his spare time.'

'That's not it!' Charlie threw a handful of sand at Izzie's green toenails.

'Hey!' gasped Izzie. 'Those weren't dry yet. Now I'll have to start all over again. Or do you think I want blobby toenails?'

'Anything is better than that mouldy green,' replied Charlie.

Izzie stuck her tongue out at her. 'You don't know what you're talking about. But go on, who's the ghost?'

Charlie shook her head. 'I'm not telling yet. I haven't got any evidence. Just a hunch, you know?'

'Oh, well, suit yourself,' sighed Izzie. 'Maybe you'll find some evidence tonight. I'm sure the ghost will put in a farewell appearance.'

'I'm absolutely certain it will.' Charlie looked at the hostel. 'I wonder what the boys are doing. They'd better not be putting any lugworms in our beds.'

'No way!' Izzie rubbed her sandy toenails. 'They've got other things on their minds. I bet they're running around trying to find a TV.'

'I'll think I'll go and check anyway.' Charlie got up and brushed the sand from her jeans.

There were few things as boring to Charlie as hanging around on a beach. Weeding her gran's garden was one of them, and she had to do that quite often enough.

Charlie ran through the hostel's entrance hall. She looked at the large clock. Half past two already. There wasn't much time till kick-off. As she raced up the stairs she heard Olly's voice. Charlie ducked down as she sneaked up the last steps and peered around the corner. There they were. All of them together, looking guilty. Charlie recognised that look a mile off. But the Piranhas weren't standing by the C.H.I.X.'s door. They were outside Mr Dudman's room. Will and Freddie had their backs to her, keeping their eyes on the corridor, while Olly and Tom were kneeling in front of the door, fiddling with the handle.

'Come on, Olly!' said Freddie out of the corner of his mouth.

'We shouldn't be doing this,' said Will. He was shifting his weight from foot to foot. 'Seriously, Freddie. This is breaking in. Olly won't be able to magic us out of this one. If my dad hears about it he'll thump me.'

'If you weren't up for it, you should've stayed in the room,' hissed Freddie. 'Didn't I say that before?'

'Done it!' squeaked Olly.

Mr Dudman's door opened. Tom nipped inside, and quickly came out again holding an Mp3 player.

Charlie held her breath. Had they gone completely mad?

'Wow, it's a real little beauty!' whispered Will. 'It's got a radio and everything.' Then he took a step back and raised his hands. 'Man, you've got to put that back. If anything happens to it, we'll all be kicked out of school.'

'Who's going to find us in the broom cupboard?' said Freddie. 'And we don't all have to sit and listen to it the whole time. One of us stays on the beach and keeps an eye on Dudman. We swap every fifteen minutes. Quarter past five, right after the final whistle, Olly takes it back to Dudman's room. Agreed?'

'Agreed,' said Olly.

Hiding their booty carefully, the Piranhas all scuttled towards the stairs.

That's when Charlie popped up.

'Oh my word,' she said. 'You've really lost the plot this time.'

The Piranhas turned as white as sheets.

'Charlie!' gasped Freddie.

'She's going to tell on us!' squeaked Olly. 'And we'll all get expelled.'

Tom was nervously licking his lips. And Will looked as if he might faint at any moment.

'I'm not going to tell!' said Charlie gruffly. 'But you should take that thing back right away. If Dudman catches you, you're dead.'

'We're just borrowing it,' said Freddie. 'For the game. We'll take it right back afterwards.'

'You're completely stark raving mad!' Charlie spun around on her heels. 'Totally gaga. But I never saw you.'

'So? Any worms in our beds?' asked Izzie after Charlie had returned to the beach. She'd put on her clothes again. 'It's a bit too cold for a bikini,' she said. 'Look at them, over there, playing in that icy water, they must have Eskimo blood or something.'

'The boys have taken Mr Dudman's Mp3 player,' said Charlie.

Izzie looked at her, amazed.

'No way!'

'I know!' Charlie let herself drop into the sand next to Izzie. 'Just so they can listen to a stupid football match. And now they're all sitting round it in some broom cupboard. Crazy or what?'

'Where is Dudman?' asked Izzie. 'I haven't seen him for ages.'

'I have,' muttered Charlie. 'He's put on a really stupid apron and he's over by the picnic spot, barbecuing sausages.'

'Does Olly know?' said Izzie. 'Who'd have thought he'd rather sit in a broom cupboard instead of scoffing sausages? They really are football crazy!'

'All the more for us, then,' said Charlie. 'Those sausages smell pretty good. How about we get ourselves some? Xa, Hannah and Helena are already in line at the barbecue. Or are your toenails still not dry?'

For that, Izzie chased Charlie all the way over to the others.

Hannah said no to the sausages, and nibbled on some salad instead. Of course, Olly magically appeared and helped himself to a huge plate of food. He worked his way through one sausage after another while keeping half an eye on Mr Dudman, but the teacher was fully occupied with keeping the cooking going. After fifteen minutes Tom appeared, looking rather glum, and took Olly's place.

'What are they going to do if Dudman goes upstairs?' mumbled Helena through a mouthful of food. Charlie had filled them all in on the Piranhas' game. 'Are they going to distract him or something?'

Hannah nearly choked on a lettuce leaf.

After Tom, it was Will's turn, and then came Olly

again. Freddie, the boss, had clearly decided he was too important to swap. Typical.

Meanwhile a charcoal-smudged and sweating Mr Dudman had sat down at a table with Mrs Rose. He was drinking a Coke and eating a sausage, as he recovered from the heat of the barbecue.

Suddenly Helena gave Charlie a nudge. 'Oh no! He's looking for something to wipe his face with. See?'

Mr Dudman was hunting through his pockets and looking round the table. He muttered something to Mrs Rose and then got to his feet.

'Oh, no, he might go to his room!' cried Hannah. The C.H.I.X. looked at Olly, but he was too busy helping himself to a third round of sausages.

Mr Dudman squeezed past Mrs Rose.

'Quick, do something – they'll get in such trouble if they're caught!' breathed Xa.

Olly was still distracted.

Charlie quickly jumped up. 'Mr Dudman!' she called.

Mr Dudman turned around.

Olly gave a start, dropped his half-eaten sausage and rushed off.

'I just wanted to ask you something, Sir.' Charlie looked the teacher straight in the eye. 'Do you think the ghost will come back tonight?'

Mr Dudman looked at Charlie for a moment. Then

the left corner of his mouth curled up into a small smile. 'I'm certain of it!' he said. 'Considering what happened last night.'

Charlie was still looking at him. 'If it does, I hope it'll stick around a bit longer than it did then.'

Mr Dudman shrugged. 'Who knows? Maybe howling and moaning and scratching at doors is all it can do. I'm no expert on such things, just a humble teacher.'

He turned around to continue making his way indoors.

'Mr Dudman!' called Hannah this time. 'Do you need something to wipe your face and hands with?'

Mr Dudman turned back to the girls again.

'Er, yes. That's very kind of you, Hannah,' he said, as she handed him a slightly grubby tissue. 'Save my poor old legs.'

'Exactly!' said Charlie. 'You want to keep your strength up for the disco tonight.'

The teacher raised an eyebrow and sat down next to Mrs Rose again.

'Phew, that was close,' breathed Helena.

'You can say that again!' Izzie rolled her eyes. 'Those idiots definitely owe us one.'

At that moment, Tom appeared with a sheepish Olly close behind. He walked over to the C.H.I.X.'s table.

'Hey.' Izzie nudged Xa. 'Another love note on its way?'

Xa blushed, but it was Charlie's ear that Tom whispered into.

'Freddie says you should come up.'

'Why?' Charlie gave him a wary look. 'Trying to boss me around as well now, is he?'

Tom made a face. 'Could you just come with me, please?'

'Where? To the broom cupboard?' Charlie shot a quick look at Mr Dudman, but he was busying himself with the barbecue.

'Yes, we found something interesting, and Freddie thinks you should listen to it.'

'Eh?' Charlie wasn't sure how seriously to take this.

'So, are you coming, or not?' Tom drummed his fingers on the table.

Charlie got up with a sigh. 'OK, OK. But if I'm not back down here in ten minutes, the others will come and get me. Understood?'

Tom just nodded. He quickly ran on ahead, back into the hostel, until they were standing in front of a narrow door. Charlie could faintly hear voices behind it. Tom knocked twice, and then once more. The door opened and they were quickly pulled into the darkness.

The Piranhas were crammed like sardines around Mr Dudman's Mp3 player.

'What's the score?' asked Tom.

'You don't want to know!' answered Will. 'It's a total disaster.'

'What do you want me for?' interrupted Charlie, impatiently.

'I want you to hear something,' said Freddie. 'As a little thank-you for not grassing on us.'

'It's quite a big thank-you, if you ask me,' growled Will. 'Not that anybody ever does.'

Freddie cleared his throat. 'We found this recording when we were mucking about,' he said, and pressed Play.

Ben Penmarric's ghost howled and moaned out of Mr Dudman's Mp3 player.

Charlie grinned.

'I knew it!' she said smugly.

'What?' Freddie looked crestfallen. 'You're not surprised?'

Charlie shook her head. 'I worked it out, but I had no proof.'

'Well, we worked it out, too, and we found the proof,' grumbled Will. 'Dudman is the ghost, and so we, the Piranhas, have won the bet.'

'You can't actually prove anything,' said Charlie. 'Unless you want me to go to Dudman and say: "Guess what we found out when the boys broke into your room and took your Mp3 player?"'

'She's right,' said Freddie hastily. 'But at least we know now who's been playing tricks on us. That's something, isn't it?'

'Definitely,' nodded Charlie, grinning. 'I wonder when he's going to use it next? Thanks for letting me listen. But now I'd really like to get out of this smelly little cupboard.'

'And I want to hear the end of the game!' said Tom.

'OK, OK!' Freddie logged back on – and a deafening yell of 'GOOOAAAAAAL!' flooded the little cupboard.

'Who's scored?' Olly nearly swallowed his tongue with excitement. 'Who's scored?'

Charlie quickly made her exit.

## Chapter
## Twenty-two

'**D**udman!' Izzie was leaning over Hannah, snipping away at her fringe. 'I still can't believe it.'

Xa was standing in front of them, holding up Izzie's travel mirror. Hannah peered into it as her hair got shorter and shorter.

'OK, just a little hair gel,' said Izzie, 'and you'll look fab.'

Hannah looked a bit unsure, especially when it turned out that none of them had any.

'But I've got lip gloss,' Izzie said. 'And eye liner, and a little bit of mascara. What do you think?'

'Um . . .' mumbled Hannah. 'I think I'd rather stay the way I am.'

Suddenly, Helena rushed into the room, totally out of breath.

'Guess what I've just found! Dudman's going to use his Mp3 player again! I went to put something in the rubbish bin outside, and saw it tucked behind one of the bins. He must've hidden it there. The bins are right next to the path we'll take when we walk back tonight. You'd never know it was there if you didn't know where to look. But now I know exactly where it is!' She plonked herself down on a chair. 'So what do we do about it?'

'Hmm . . . I've got an idea.' Charlie was sitting on her top bunk, dangling her feet. 'But we'll need the boys.'

The others looked at her in surprise.

Charlie explained her plan and Helena was despatched to see the Piranhas. Will was going to have a star part to play.

The disco was taking place in an outbuilding which stood at a distance from the hostel and was perfect for noisy events. Inside there was a small dance floor, surrounded by tables and chairs. There were tatty posters on the wall, and an old stereo with a CD player and a turntable, but no iPod dock, noted Olly. The lighting consisted of some bright overhead lights above the DJ and red spotlights around the room. Next to the stereo was a pile of CDs. The teachers had brought drinks, and there were bags of crisps to eat, though most of the class were still stuffed from Mr Dudman's sausage feast.

The C.H.I.X. were the last to arrive. After they'd finished preparing for Charlie's plan, Izzie had scrounged some hair gel for Hannah from the girls next door. The result wasn't bad at all. After that, Izzie had tried on three outfits before Xa and Charlie had grabbed her suitcase and locked it in the wardrobe. The other C.H.I.X. went dressed as they were, their chicken feathers around their necks, and with sand from the beach still stuck to their jeans.

Charlie did notice, though, that Xa smelled sweeter than before. Izzie, of course, always smelled gorgeous. As the girls walked into the party, they immediately saw the Piranhas. The four boys were in a good mood, for the broom-cupboard goal had been scored by their team. Even Will was looking happier than usual, though that might have had less to do with the football results than with the fact that Charlie had given him the most important part in her plan. Olly was wearing a hat, while Freddie had hung a tiny dried crab from the earring that all the Piranhas wore. It made him look like a pirate.

'Where's Tom?' asked Xa.

'Somewhere behind that pile of CDs,' replied Will. 'He's got a slot as DJ.'

'Oh.' Xa fiddled with her chicken feather. 'I'll just go and say hello to him.' She gave Charlie a quick glance before pushing her way through the crowd towards the DJ platform.

'He's written her at least four notes,' whispered Izzie.

'Four?' Charlie shook her head. 'I only saw one.'

'Charlie!' Izzie arched her eyebrows. 'You never notice these things.'

'Hey, Hannah,' said Olly. 'We've, erm, got something for you.' He took off his hat, reached inside, and – 'Abracadabra!' – produced a necklace made of seashells. 'It's a charm to ward off bad stuff. Works nearly one hundred per cent of the time.'

'Oh, thanks!' breathed Hannah. She put the necklace over her head, taking care not to mess up her new hair. She smiled happily. 'I really don't know what to say.'

'That's OK,' said Freddie. 'Will made it. Just like my earring.' He pointed to his earlobe.

'Wow!' said Izzie. 'I'd love one of those.'

'No problem!' mumbled Will, looking awkwardly at his hands.

'And what about our bet?' Olly asked.

Charlie shrugged. 'I'd say it's a tie. We're kind of on the same team now, aren't we?'

'Then how about this,' suggested Freddie. 'If we carry your bags to the train, we get to dance with our favourite C.H.I.X.?'

'Sounds good.' Izzie batted her eyelids so hard that

Charlie could hardly bear to look at her. She felt herself blush all the way up to the roots of her hair, but luckily nobody could see in the dim light.

Hannah chewed her lip. 'That probably means you all want to dance with Izzie.'

'Not necessarily.' Olly laughed slightly nervously.

'It wouldn't work anyway,' said Charlie abruptly. 'There's five of us, and only four of you. That means one of us will get left out. That's not fair.'

'Well, I don't mind dancing with two of you!' said Olly. He was feeling quite bold this evening.

Charlie looked at the others.

'It's fine by me,' said Izzie.

'Me, too,' said Helena.

Hannah just nodded.

'OK.' Charlie sighed. 'Whatever. We all know who Tom's going to pick, anyway.' She looked around. Xa hadn't come back yet, though Tom was busy at the turntables.

Suddenly, the bright overhead lights went off and the music started up so loudly that Mrs Rose nearly fell off her chair.

Olly pushed back his hat. He held out his left hand to Helena, and his right hand to Hannah, and led them to the dance floor, now bathed in a red glow.

Will looked at Izzie, looked away again, and then looked at her again. He couldn't get a word out.

Izzie giggled and tossed back her hair. 'Well, do you want to dance or not?' she asked him.

Will muttered something indecipherable. Then the two of them disappeared off to the dance floor as well. That just left Freddie and Charlie standing between the empty tables.

'Bad luck, it looks like you got me,' muttered Charlie.

'So?' asked Freddie. 'It was you I wanted to dance with.'

'What?' asked Charlie.

Tom cranked up the volume even more.

'I wanted to dance with you anyway!' Freddie yelled in her ear. 'But I warn you, I'm rubbish at dancing.'

'So am I!' Charlie screamed back.

And they both laughed, and then they danced together anyway.

The disco was supposed to finish at ten, when the room needed to be locked up again. But at five to ten, the electricity suddenly cut out, pitching everything into darkness. 'Don't panic!' came Mr Dudman's voice. 'We probably just blew a fuse. Let's all quietly and calmly go outside.'

Whispering, everybody felt their way through the narrow doorway. Neither Freddie nor Charlie could make out any of their friends in the dark.

'Ha! This must be the start of Dudman's final ghost show,' whispered Freddie in Charlie's ear. 'I bet he fiddled with the electricity to make it all more spooky.'

'Just as well we got ready before the disco,' Charlie whispered back. She held on to Freddie's sleeve, so they wouldn't get split up. 'Good old Dudman is going to have the surprise of his life.'

'I think we'd better all go back to the hostel,' Mrs Rose called out. 'We were going to clean up tomorrow anyway, but I'd better tell the caretaker about the fuse.'

'No, I'll do that!' said Mr Dudman quickly. He strode off in the direction of the hostel. Nobody paid him any attention except the C.H.I.X. and the Piranhas, who watched him leave.

Sure enough, halfway to the hostel in the darkness ahead, Mr Dudman disappeared between the rubbish bins.

'I bet he's going to turn it on now,' Freddie whispered to Charlie as they waited with the others.

'Look, he's coming back already,' said Tom. 'Showtime!'

Mr Dudman was strolling back, his face a picture of innocence. The crowd of children pushed past him, laughing and shouting. They were just a few metres away from the rubbish bins.

'What's that?!' someone called out. 'I can hear something. Listen. It's the ghost!'

It was the same howling and moaning that they had heard at the beach the previous night. Everybody froze and listened.

Then, suddenly, the groaning stopped and instead a deep voice growled: 'Duuuuudmaaan! Duuuudmaaan, where are yooooou?'

Everybody turned to look at Mr Dudman, who stood frozen in shock.

Xa had to press her hand over her mouth to stop herself from laughing out loud.

'Dudman!' the creepy voice continued. 'You have disturbed my rest!'

'Wow, Will,' whispered Izzie. 'You sound brilliant!'

'You sound really scary!' agreed Helena.

'Like a zombie or something,' Hannah nodded in agreement. 'I've got goosebumps all over.'

The others obviously felt the same. Nobody had moved. Nobody ran towards the voice, to see where it was coming from. Not even Mrs Rose.

'Dudmaaaan! I am warning youuuu!' carried on the raspy voice. 'If you make these poor, innocent children write essays about me, or the museum or the environment or anything else boring at all, I will visit you one night and throttle you with my bony hands.'

'OK, OK, I give up!' called Mr Dudman. He raised his hands in surrender. 'I admit it all! I was the ghost. OK?'

'You?' Mrs Rose looked astonished. 'It was you all along? Scratching at doors, that creepy laugh, the howling at the beach? For goodness' sake!'

Mr Dudman nodded. 'Guilty as charged! The coins and the wet footprints and even the bits of fabric were mine, too. I did plant some more things, but nobody found those.'

Mrs Rose started to laugh. She laughed so hard that she gave herself hiccups.

Will's voice was still moaning in the background. Charlie ran to the rubbish bins and switched off the player. Mrs Rose was still giggling when Charlie got back.

'You of all people, Mr Dudman!' she said. 'You of all people!'

'What do you mean, me of all people?' Mr Dudman looked a bit hurt.

'It was so mean of you!' Mrs Rose pursed her lips. They were coral red tonight. 'It was so mean of you . . . not to let me in on the joke and help you!'

Mr Dudman looked completely floored.

'I would have had some first-class haunting ideas,' continued Mrs Rose. 'Without question. I am deeply hurt that you left me out of everything. How are you going to make up for this?'

Abashed, Mr Dudman pushed his hand through his thinning hair. 'I don't know. Maybe we can think of something on the next school trip?'

'A bit feeble, but OK.' Mrs Rose nodded at him. 'I will be sure to remind you.'

'Mr Dudman!' said Freddie. 'Does Ben Penmarric really haunt St Peter's Island? Or was that all made up?'

'No, no, he really is supposed to haunt these parts.' Mr Dudman tugged his earlobe. 'I just moved him here from the other side of the island.' He shrugged. 'Call it artistic licence.'

Helena looked at Mr Dudman with round eyes. 'He's actually out there, haunting the other side of the island?'

The Piranhas groaned.

'Don't worry about it, Helena,' said Charlie.

'Sorry, but I have to ask.' Mr Dudman looked around. 'Who found out first? Was it the C.H.I.X. or the Piranhas?'

Charlie and Freddie looked at each other.

'It was all of us,' said Freddie. 'We did it together.'

'Indeed? Is that so? How interesting.' Mr Dudman smiled his most self-satisfied teacher's smile. 'Then that just leaves one question. Whose creepy voice did we just hear, if it wasn't old Penmarric's?'

'That was Will,' said Izzie. 'He was good, wasn't he?'

'He was!' Mrs Rose gave Will a look of surprise. 'You seem to have hidden some real talent from us, Will.'

'Not really . . .' muttered Will. He looked as if he'd

like to burrow into the sand and disappear.

'Yes, really. It was quite exceptional,' Mr Dudman chimed in. 'You're clearly much more talented than me. We should recruit you for the drama club.'

Will squirmed with embarrassment.

'And who wrote the script?' asked Mrs Rose.

'Charlie,' said Helena. 'She wrote it all down, we found the player behind the bins . . .'

'. . . which made things much easier than we expected,' interrupted Freddie.

'And then,' continued Helena, 'we just recorded over Mr Dudman's howling and moaning.'

'Yeah. They're not as stupid as they look,' came a voice from behind them.

Charlie turned around. It was Ellie. When she noticed Charlie looking at her she quickly pulled a face.

'All right!' Mrs Rose clapped her hands. 'I say we now all get our heads down for a good night's sleep. OK? After all, we have to get back on that horrid boat tomorrow.'

'Oh, no!' moaned Hannah. 'Did she have to remind me? Now she's ruined the whole evening.'

'Nuh-uh!' Izzie put her arm around Hannah's shoulders. 'We'll distract you. You'll see.'

## Chapter Twenty-three

The C.H.I.X. didn't go to sleep. While Ellie snored happily in her bed, the five girls sat on Charlie's top bunk, eating crisps and chocolate, and looked at the sea. They had opened the window wide so that they could get a farewell sniff of the salty air. As the room got colder, they just huddled closer together for warmth.

'I wish time would stop right now,' said Hannah, quietly. 'Just for, like, a week or so.'

Xa nodded. 'You know what I sometimes wish? That you could bottle moments like this. Then when you're sad, you could just open the lid and get a noseful of happiness.'

'That would be brilliant,' said Charlie. 'We could have a whole shelf full of jars. One for the school trip, a Christmas jar, one full of sunshine, one full of snow . . .'

'And a big jar of C.H.I.X. adventures,' added Helena.

They sat in silence a bit longer, looking at the water. The rhythmic sound of the waves soon made them sleepy. Izzie was the first to yawn. She put her head on Hannah's shoulder.

'Oh no,' sighed Hannah. 'I just remembered that awful ferry.'

'Keep your eye on the horizon at all times,' murmured Izzie. 'Always helps.'

'And how did you keep your eye on the horizon while you were below deck playing on the fruit machines?' asked Charlie sleepily.

'Got me!' sniggered Izzie. 'But I hear it works brilliantly.'

'Who told you that?' asked Helena.

Izzie brushed a stray lock of hair from her face and yawned. 'Freddie and Will.'

Helena rolled her eyes. 'They know it all, those two.'

'Xa?' asked Izzie. 'You and Tom, are you going out now?'

Xa didn't answer. She lay curled up like a kitten between the others, fast asleep.

'We'll have to get Helena to spy on them for us,' said Charlie. 'Or we'll never find out.'

Helena folded her arms and frowned. 'I'd never do something like that. Ever!'

'Don't worry!' Charlie nudged her. 'I was just kidding.'

'Ssh!' Izzie gestured towards Ellie's bed. 'Listen to her snoring.'

'That's nothing! You talk in your sleep,' replied Charlie.

'I so don't!' Izzie fiddled with her hair. 'You're just winding me up.'

'No, it's true!' Now it was Hannah's turn to snigger. 'I've heard you, too.'

Izzie blushed.

Charlie put an arm around her shoulder. 'I just couldn't make out what you were saying,' she whispered in her ear. 'Which was really annoying.'

'She giggles in her sleep, too,' said Hannah.

'Well, do you know what you do?' asked Izzie. 'You pull your duvet right up to your nose so your feet poke out at the bottom. And Charlie rolls around so much in her sleep that she ends up completely uncovered with her cuddly chicken on her face.'

They all nearly fell off the bed with laughter, while Xa slept on peacefully through it all.

'And me?' Helena looked eagerly at the others. 'What do I do?'

'You?' Charlie got to her knees, pushed her face into

the pillow and stuck her bum in the air. 'You do this.'

'Stop it! Stop!' gasped Izzie. 'That's exactly what she does.'

That was when Xa finally woke up. She rubbed her eyes and mumbled: 'What are you laughing about? Nothing about me, I hope.'

'No,' replied Charlie. 'You sleep perfectly normally. Like a little kitten.'

'That's good.' Xa closed her eyes again and curled herself up even more. 'Tell me when we're there,' she mumbled. 'This stupid boat is really rocking.'

Well, that did it.

Helena was laughing so hard that Izzie only just managed to stop her rolling off the bed.

'There's a jar we forgot,' said Hannah when they'd all managed to calm down a little. 'A jar full of laughter!'

'No room for any of Tom's jokes in there, then,' said Charlie.

'Oh, stop it!' Hannah rubbed her face. 'All this laughing is making my cheeks ache.'

'I once read about a man who laughed himself to death,' said Helena.

'What a great way to go!' Charlie took her cuddly hen and snuggled up next to Xa. She closed her eyes. 'This really was a great trip,' she murmured. 'I just hope Dudman doesn't spoil everything and make us write an essay about it.'

'I expect he will,' said Izzie, yawning. 'Could some-one close the window?'

But the others were already fast asleep, Xa and Charlie with their heads at one end of the bunk bed, Helena and Hannah at the other.

Izzie yawned again as she climbed down and tiptoed to the window. She took one more look at the sea and then crawled back in with the others. She found herself a tiny free spot, with Hannah's toes under her nose and Charlie's elbow in her back. And then she too was soon fast asleep.